Knock ~~Twice~~

25 modern folk tales for troubling times

Edited by Andrew Simms

THE REAL PRESS/New Weather Institute

www.therealpress.co.uk/www.newweather.org

Published in 2017 by the Real Press with the New Weather Institute.
www.therealpress.co.uk

ISBN (print) 978-1978124165
ISBN (ebook) 978-0995662339

Contents

Cover illustration by Annes Stevens.

"We sense new weather
We are on our marks
We are all in this together"

Carol Ann Duffy

Foreword

'The last person on earth sat alone in a room, and there was a knock at the door...' Want to know what happened next? So do I.

Now what about this: 'On a particular day, the concentration of the greenhouse gas, carbon dioxide, in the atmosphere, was 403.28 parts per million.' Is the curiosity quite the same? Less so, I suspect, even for those of us who care passionately about our destabilising climate. Stories, more than facts, hold our attention and pattern our lives. Facts we can deny, stories slip passed our ideological guard into the imagination.

In stories, we make sense of the world, and find ways to deal with what doesn't make sense. They let us imagine how things can be different, helping them become so. It doesn't take many words. 'For sale, baby shoes, never worn,' has been called the saddest story written. Margaret Atwood's, 'Longed for him. Got him. Shit,' needs no elaboration. And, Eileen Gunn's six word story: 'Computer, did we bring batteries? Computer?' in all its brevity detonates a tension at the heart of human progress. Love allowed in. Demons cast out. Questions raised.

We live within stories. Too often, though, they are written by people and powers that do not have our interests, nor the interests of the great diversity of life on earth, at heart. The stories we hear loudest and most frequently in our daily lives, come from, or echo, media dominated by voices who represent an economic status quo. These, to a greater or lesser degree, either ignore or explain away the unfortunate inevitability of worsening inequality, poverty and environmental collapse.

In this book, people struggling to solve these problems set out to tell better tales. For decades, campaigners for social and ecological progress have exhibited a stoic faith in the power of statistics and rational argument to win change. There have been wins, new rights for vulnerable groups and protection for other species, but now we teeter on a greater precipice.

Knock knock...

Ten years on from the great financial crisis of 2007-08, confidence has leaked from the mainstream, neo-liberal economic model like air from a balloon long after the party has ended. In response, optimistic, new, and often youth-driven movements have revived grassroots activism where before disconnection and alienation were draped like a shroud over the body politic. But equally, there have been opposite, reactionary backlashes, such as the election of Donald Trump as US president seeking greater isolation from the world, and Britain's narrow vote, quickly regretted, seeking greater isolation from Europe.

In the gap between the collapse of one story about our economic possibilities, used to explain and justify countless cruelties, and the emergence of another, or others, that could either provoke us to turn against each other, or help us all thrive, together within planetary environmental boundaries, sit flux and uncertainty.

Here, then, are some new and original tales from people of goodwill. Each is a practice in better understanding our errors, and a rehearsal of the journey towards making things right. The need for creative experimentation is clear. It is impossible to know in advance what will grab human imaginations. How often are we caught unaware by what becomes a lightning conductor for change. In stories we reveal what we value, articulate our fears and can glimpse better worlds that then, we can at least walk towards.

In reflecting on how he solved some of the questions of our very existence, Albert Einstein commented that: 'When I examine myself and my methods of thought, I come to the conclusion that the gift of fantasy has meant more to me than any talent for abstract, positive thinking.' He is also credited with observing that: 'If you want your children to be intelligent, read them fairytales. If you want them to be more intelligent, read them more fairytales.'

I cannot promise anything, but I am prepared to bet, that if you knock twice on the cover of this book, and then read from the beginning to the end, when you next reach your hand into your pocket of ideas, you will find something new and useful that wasn't there before.

Andrew Simms
October 2017

1

All the words of all the worlds

Jan Dean

In a small house in a small garden on the edge of the city, there lived a wise woman. Sometimes people came to sit with her – to ask advice, to talk, to listen and the wise woman did what she could to answer their questions, although often her answer was: 'I do not know'.

Some found this strange and disappointing, but others found comfort in seeing that knowledge and wisdom are not the same thing.

One day a baby was left on her doorstep. A tiny scrap of a thing who cried with a fierce energy, her face screwed into a furious red landscape of creases and folds. 'Whose child is this?' the neighbours asked. 'Who has left this squalling baby here?'

'I do not know,' said the wise woman and picked up the baby, took her in and found milk and clean linen.

Days passed and weeks and months and years but

no-one ever came to claim the child and so she became the daughter of the wise woman, but they were very unalike. The girl was restless and discontented. She spoke before she thought and she acted before she thought of thinking. But although other people looked sideways at the girl and shook their heads, the wise woman never did. 'The child has a hole in her life,' the wise woman said. 'She has questions that cannot be answered and who knows what that will do in a child's heart?'

Well, this girl's heart grew greedy. Not for apples or honey or cake, but for knowledge. 'School is a well,' she said, 'and I will drink it dry. Knowledge is power and I will learn everything there is to know. And when I know everything, I will be happy. But where to start? The world is large and full of wonders.'

'Ah,' said the wise woman and gave the girl a peach, and the girl smiled and ate it without ever seeing the sunset colours of its skin, or noticing the fuzz of it upon her lips. 'Ah,' sighed the wise woman and closed her eyes.

So the girl set off on her search to know all things. And she did see wonders, but she was not happy. *Knowledge is power.* She said to herself, but although she knew more and more she did not feel powerful. Then one morning she woke with an idea bright in her head. 'I will learn the meaning of every word that is. Every word that has ever been spoken and maybe some that only live in silence... for are not all things bound by words? So if I know the meaning of all words I will surely know all things... and if I know all things I will have all power.... and when I have all power I can do all things... and then I will be content.'

And oh, it was such a powerful thought, and so full of need and greed that it moved through the air like a pulse and the throb of it woke a sleeping thing deep in the heart of the dark inside a mountain. And the sleeping thing stretched its scaly arms and blinked its glassy eyes and yawned a lazy-hungry yawn, before it rose from its bed and with its long flickering tongue licked itself into a shape more suited for meeting people than its true shape.

So it was on her journey through the land of lakes and forests that the girl met the beautiful woman with the shiny golden casket.

'Oh, it's you,' the beautiful woman said. 'I heard you calling me and now we meet at last.'

The girl was puzzled by this greeting, and questions rose in her head, but she was dazzled, too, by the shiny golden casket and soon the shine of it had wiped her question clean away. All she wanted was to hold that lovely box, to open its precious lid, and own whatever sweet, exquisite treasure lay inside.

'It is your heart's desire,' the beautiful woman said.

And the great emptiness in the girl's heart cried out for it and sent a wave of feeling so great that the beautiful woman shuddered at the strength of it and for a second her disguise wavered.

'What...?' the girl gasped.

But the creature from the night inside the mountain was once again composed inside its beautiful disguise and the girl's eyes were on the glistening casket and she was beguiled.

'In here are all the words of all the worlds that ever were. All the words and all their meanings... I have travelled far to give you this,' the beautiful woman said, 'but now that I am here I cannot bear to part with it.'

Then the girl grew angry. Everything she longed for was within her reach. How dare this woman try to keep it from her?

And the beautiful woman saw the anger blossom in the young girl's eyes and felt her arrogance like heat from a fire.

'I will take the golden casket as my right,' she thought. 'I will know all things, have all power.'

Oh, how that young girl's heart filled with rage,

how resolute it grew – how implacable. And how that creature from the night within the mountain smiled as it felt the young girl's heart turn stonier and stonier in her dark determination to have the golden casket and its contents.

'Why, my dear,' the monster inside the beautiful disguise whispered, 'we could be sisters, you and I. You grow more like me by the minute. And of course you must have my casket, but as a keepsake I must have just one word, or else I cannot part with it.'

And the girl was so eager to grasp the casket that she readily agreed.

Years passed. The girl became a woman and her knowledge of all things brought her great power and great wealth and her favourite of all the words in all the worlds was *more*. And the more she had the less everyone else had. Soon she ruled the world like a great jewelled beetle sitting on a giant pile of dung.

But she was not happy. So at last she travelled back through the smoking wasteland of so many kingdoms, ignoring the outstretched hands of beggars, protected from the starving hoards by her gleaming soldiers, until at last she reached the small house on the edge of the city where the wise woman lived. And what a mean hovel it was. She found it hard to believe she had ever lived in such a place.

But as she walked through the green garden she

did remember the kindness of the wise woman and when she saw her again she felt a small crack in the hard and stony shell around her heart. And so she told her story to the wise woman and was appalled and amazed when the wise woman wept.

'Oh, little one,' she said in the midst of her tears. 'How you were tricked by the one who offered you that casket. For the word she kept is the one which holds the welfare of all people in its meaning. Unless you treasure it you can never be happy. Unless you treasure it no-one can be happy. Come here, come close and let me say the word that wicked creature kept from you.'

Then the wise woman leant close to her lost daughter and whispered: 'Enough.'

2

The God App

Nick Robins

Steve was restless. 'Oh my God', he sighed. "Why is everything going wrong?'

'Look within and you will find the answer,' came a husky voice from his jacket pocket.

'What do you mean?' replied Steve – and then quickly stopped: he was talking to himself; things were really getting out of hand.

Reaching into his jacket, he took out his phone, hoping someone, somewhere would have tagged him, liked him, retweeted him.

On the chessboard of apps that sprang to life, just next to the Weather, he noticed a new one, black and white, simply saying GOD (admittedly in Gothic script).

He tapped it and out came that same husky voice, a lovely molasses of a baritone.

'I told you, didn't I – look within your jacket and you'll find me. Well, here I am.'

Steve had never got the hang of these digital

helpers with their jaunty names and stale tones.

'Ok, but I didn't ask for you and I don't need another bloody app wasting my time and money,' moaned Steve.

'Not so fast, my son,' said the app. 'I distinctly heard you calling me. I know this is not my usual incarnation, but you've got to move with the times.'

'What do you mean incarnation? Isn't that some Hindu thing? My mate Hari was telling me about Krishna in the pub yesterday.'

'It's all very simple – it means when the spirit becomes flesh though, as a vegetarian, I don't like the carnivorous connotations,' breezed the phone.

'But you're not flesh. You're just a programme in the cloud,' retorted Steve.

'Well, it's better than people thinking I actually live on a cloud!' chuckled the app.

This banter was going nowhere.

'So, who are you and how are you going to help me?' asked Steve grumpily.

'I'm God of course – who else? I will be with you every step,' replied the app, suddenly quite assertive.

'I don't believe in God – religion's just mumbo jumbo and massacres. Goodbye, my friend, I'm going to swipe you to kingdom...'

But before Steve could finish his sentence, the phone blazed bright white and wriggled out of his hand. But it didn't fall to the pavement, just hovered before Steve's gawping face.

'It's not a question of belief, I'm afraid. I am the great I Am whether you choose to pay attention or not,' said God.

Now the app filled the whole phone and the phone had grown so it was taller than Steve's big brother Paul.

'Keep your hair on,' croaked Steve, wracking his brains to think how he could get out of this.

'So who created you?' he asked, somewhat sheepishly.

Silence. Silence that seemed to last for a very long time, until the floating phone, perked up and said:

'The earliest thing I can remember is creating the universe – being that force of love that drives all energy and all living things. But, however hard I try, I can't remember anything before the Big Bang.'

'Aha, said Steve. 'Gotcha! That could just be a memory programmed for you by some spotty nerd in Finland!'

'I'm sad to hear you say that Steve. I was so looking forward to our time together.'

Suddenly, the app went blank, the phone just

shrank and it lay there in Steve's hand, its battery completely drained.

'Damn,' he said. 'How in God's name am I going to find my way home without my phone?'

'Do you want another go?' whispered the app.

3
Little England Gothic
Suki Ferguson

There was a knock at the door. Lynn sat up at the kitchen table, alert. She had been drowsing over a cup of tea and the morning's paper. The next clue in the crossword was a real stumper and her thoughts had drifted. Stiffly, she got up from her chair and looked out of the window towards the quiet lane. No unfamiliar car to be seen. Who could it be? She felt her heart jump a little after the slow hours alone.

'Coming.'

Whoever it was waited patiently. From the hallway, Lynn could see that there were two figures, standing tall and still, shadowed in the rippled glass. She frowned as she opened the door.

'Hello?'

A smart-looking woman and a young man in a suit smiled from the doorstep.

'Hello!' said the young man. 'Mrs Littlebury? My name is Chris, and this is Mary. We're here to introduce ourselves and talk with you. It's about the upcoming election. Would you have a moment to chat? It'll only take a minute."

"Hmm. Aren't you a bit young for a politician?"

Mary leaned in to answer, holding her clipboard up between Chris and her with a conspiratorial air. "That's a fair question, Mrs Littlebury. He's not standing, but we'd love to get your thoughts on the whole thing. If you're not too busy though?"

The question hung in the air. Lynn peered at her. "Well, don't dither out there. Come in and have some tea. Help me with the crossword."

The kitchen was sweltering and spotlessly clean. Mary and Chris sat around the table, watching Lynn fill the teapot and rummage for spoons.

"I do hope you don't mind me asking, whether you have made a plan for your vote on Thursday?" Mary asked, straightening out her leaflets.

"Oh yes. Thank you." Suddenly Lynn wasn't sure what they were referring to. She resolved to give nothing away.

"I've been given to understand, Mrs Littlebury, that our candidate's policies are of special relevance to you, and we hope you'll consider a vote for him on the big day," Chris said, stirring his tea. "We can't emphasise enough how much change is needed. This parish is not would it could be. Or even what it used to be." He watched Lynn.

That sounded familiar somehow. "Quite right. When the sheep market was held here, it was altogether different. I used to see all sorts here. And there was Mrs Branton's schoolroom." She gazed at the wallpaper. "I used to walk to Mrs Branton's and back. All when I was a young girl, of course. My grandchildren live in Walford, get the bus to that smart school, The Grange." She fell quiet, then eyed Chris. "We had a donkey back then, you know. Bertram, he was called. It was Bertie for short." She waited for Chris to respond.

"Of course. Bertie." Chris paused. Mary cleared her throat. He looked over to her and she widened her eyes until her continued. "We know that things aren't right here, Mrs Littlebury. Not yet. Not for your grandchildren. But our candidate is the right man, with the right ideas. Here, let me show you what I mean."

He placed an open leaflet on the polished tabletop next to the tea things. His words flowed fast. "We know that things are strained now. You'll know from going to the local surgery, for your appointments?" Lynn nodded. Mary made a note on her clipboard.

"There's just too many people. All queuing up and eking things out, rather than giving back, contributing. What our candidate offers is a solution." The picture in the leaflet showed an imposing house, shielded from fields by a low stone wall.

'I pledge to: Bring our elders under one roof.' said the bold type below. "It's a huge step forwards," Mary said. "All the necessary comforts for those who qualify. Assessed on a lifetime contribution basis, and I'm sure, Lynn, you'd meet the mark." She smiled. "And there are other options."

Reaching out, she turned the page. "Our candidate will bring in a reform that will release elders of their duties. 'An incremental plan for public healthcare users and pension-claimants, reducing the impact on state services that high users generate,'" she read aloud, then paused at the next paragraph. "Anyway we happened to speak with the Somers family next door and they mentioned your name. There'll be tax breaks for those who volunteer first, are the first to free things up for their families, you might say." Mary folded the leaflet shut, to show the cover with a picture a brisk, smiling man in crisp white shirtsleeves.

"Our research shows that not only is it the most economically sound course for releasing untapped capital and reducing the tax burden, it will change things for *you*. And of course, you can vote for it - while, for example, your grandkids might want to, but not be able to. A mandate is what we all need. It's really quite simple. So now you understand why we stopped by, to alert you before Thursday and see what you think." She beamed at Lynn.

Lynn blinked slowly and held her china cup. Her tea was getting cold. Who were they again? They had asked her about Bertie. How was it they had known about him? Both of them were smiling in a friendly sort of way. She did like young Colin, handsome boy. Or was it Chris?

"Thank you. I do like to support local initiatives. I'm tired now. Would you mind? I need to get on." The silence was punctuated by the tick of the wall clock. Chris and Mary smiled at each other as Lynn looked down again at the leaflet before her. They scraped back their chairs and stood.

"Of course. We just wanted to say hello, outline the policies." Chris put his cup on the kitchen counter, straightened his tie. "So you are prepared for Thursday - we have high hopes. We're thrilled you're considering our candidate. We'll be back to help you get to the polling station Thursday, then?"

"Yes, yes, Thursday then." Lynn nodded, wondering why she was thinking about Bertie again all of a sudden. Dear old Bertie. They were moving away through the hallway now.

"Thank you for tea. And remember what this

village needs! Our candidate really has the best plans for you, Mrs Littlebury. The best plans!"

4

Joe and the Wail

Sarah Woods

ONE

Some stories happen once upon a time. Some time after time. Some stories are read out loud. Some whispered quietly. Others not told at all. Some stories are shared so we remember that they happened. Others in the hope they never do.

Once. On a day like all days had become, when we'd forgotten that there had been other kinds of days, a blue whale calf, finding herself separated from her mother after a meeting with a cruise ship, and confused by the water temperature, followed a warm current up a river until she scraped along the bottom. And stopped. Beached. Landed. Citied.

People came with spades to dig her out, with buckets of water to keep her wet, with fish, with placards, with cameras and microphones. People from a marine park came. People from the zoo came.

It was a time when people made something

happen by their own actions, like the journey of a whale into the heart of a city, and then said how unacceptable it was. And that it must never happen again.

A Very Important Man came with his wife. She wore a dress that nobody had ever seen her wear before. It was terrible about the whale, but she was pleased to wear the dress. The Very Important Man said:

V.I.M.: This is a big whale. This whale is historic, it's epic. And we're going to get it back and swimming. We're here to take care of this whale. And that is what we will do.

Moved by his own words, his eyes filled and a fat salt-water tear dripped first onto his cheek, then onto the nose of the whale. Sensing its element, the creature opened her mouth and gave out a wail so complete you would think her kind should be spelled that way. The water in the river rippled, the fish in the buckets flipped and loose flesh on the larger spectators vibrated. The wail marked the fall of one time and the dawn of the next.

It harboured change. Something fell from the hastily-erected staging, like a shelled pistachio, into the great wailing mouth. And then the mouth closed.

And everything was the same as before, except for one thing. The V.I.M. was gone.

As if born for that moment, ten men prized open the whale's mouth using broom handles. It was empty. And then came a tiny, a homeopathic dose of a voice. It said:

"Goot mider fook awda heer."

TWO

The first idea was to cut the whale open, to get the V.I.M. out. Tout suite. But apparently that wasn't allowed. Because the Blue Whale was a protected species and there are far fewer Blue Whales in the world than there are Very Important Men.

The V.I.M. argued, on his mobile to the Whale Expert, that everyone was free to be successful and wealthy in the world because that's how the world worked now, and that he shouldn't be penalised because Very Important Men were better at being free and successful than Blue Whales.

The second idea was to lift the whale calf by crane onto a truck and take her to a water world, which the V.I.M. would build in time for the whale to arrive, so the whale could live and he could run his world from inside her. There was a problem when he couldn't sign the contracts, but they got an ipad to him with a bucket of krill, and he did his signature electronically and emailed it. They got a laminated copy of his favourite newspaper to him. They also got a golden table lamp, a carved writing desk, a swivelly chair, a round rug and six plastic wine glasses to him in the same way. The V.I.M. took some pictures of himself and posted them on Instagram. It looked just like his office, only darker.

The final thing left to do was the branding and, after much debate, it was decided to name it:

The Very Important Authentic Whale World Excellence Land.

It didn't mean anything. But that didn't matter. Because it had all the words in it.

THREE

Blue floated in her tank, her nose touching one end and her tail the other. My job was to put sunblock on her skin with a mop, because the water wasn't deep enough to protect it. In her tank, Blue didn't look blue. More mottled grey. And she made a low sound you could hear through your feet, like a drum beating.

That morning, Blue vomited up the lamp and three plastic wine glasses. I swept them into a pile by the tank. The Whale Expert was called. She said Blue was suffering from being full of non-biodegradable stuff. That it was clogging her up. She said Blue was growing and needed more space. Soon her tongue would weigh as much as an elephant and her heart would be as big as a car. The Whale Expert said Blue was depressed. And that she shouldn't be kept in captivity. And that the drum sound was Blue calling for a friend.

The whale opened her mouth and vomited again. This time out came the writing desk, the other three plastic wine glasses, the round rug and the V.I.M.'s wallet. I swept it all into the pile. One of the Very Important Staff shouted:

O.V.I.S.: Try and get yourself vomited out, sir!

The V.I.M.'s wife came to visit. She was wearing a dress I had never seen her wear before. For a few minutes she spoke to her husband down the blowhole. She called him Joe. She was the only one who still did. Then she moved away. She seemed to be having a battle with her own face, trying to express her anguish through its pulled and plumped exterior. I asked if she was okay:

WIFE: He doesn't tell me I look beautiful anymore.
ME: Do you think that's because he can't see you?

Still her face did not, could not, betray what lay beneath. She said:

WIFE: I'm expecting a delivery.

And she went home and she never came back to The Very Important Authentic Whale World Excellence Land.

FOUR

The next morning, Blue vomited again. The third vomit produced mainly bile, together with some laminated newspapers, the swivelly chair and the V.I.M.'s shoes. The Whale Expert said that unless Blue was released, she was going to die. One of the Very Important Staff said that the Very Important Man must be cut out, before the whale died. The Whale Expert said that Blue must be put back into the sea. One of the Very Important Staff said that this was impossible. And then the V. I. M. said:

V.I.M.: Put the whale back in the sea.
O.V.I.S: But how do we get you out, sir?
V.I.M.: I've been dreaming of the sea.

The V.I.M. said he had grown to like his life inside the whale. It had given him time to think. And to not think. His staff asked him what he needed for his voyage. The V.I.M. said he needed nothing. That it was nice and spacious without all the things. And warm. And he was happy listening to the beat of Blue's heart. He was seventy years old, he said, and Blue was only about six months. With a life expectancy of eighty or ninety years, she would safely hold him for the rest of his days.

FIVE

It took a crane, two boats and fifty people to get Blue back out to sea. The V.I.M. sang Rollin' on the River for the whole time. For five hours straight. To help Blue stay calm. He did the backing vocals as well.

V.I.M.: (Sings) And we're rollin (rollin')
             Rollin (rollin' now)

Rollin on a river (rollin' on the river)

At first she floated, listless in the water, and then – sensing her freedom – she started to swim. About half a mile out, she turned and breached high. Then again. Slapping her tail.

And then Blue was gone.
And the V.I.M. was gone.

I asked One of the Very Important Man's Staff what I should do with all the stuff I had swept into a biley pile.

O.V.I.S.: Clear it up. Get rid of it.

I handed the wallet to the centre's lost property. And I took the rest home and sold it online.

Some stories we know. Some stories we know are there, but we push them to the edges of our lives, afraid of how they might change us. Other stories we don't know we don't know. And all of these stories we must seek. And all of these stories we must tell.

5
Bluebeard and Partners
Anthea Lawson

Once there was, and once there was not, a young woman from a kind-enough home in which there were not many books, who nevertheless found her way to university. She chose to study law, since she quietly knew she was clever and that she wanted to use her brain, and because it seemed like a sensible thing to do when her family didn't have any money to help her.

It was hard at first: to find friends, to learn enough to justify the debts that were growing so steadily. That first Christmas, her mother's friends thought she hadn't changed very much, really, though inside she wondered if she had. By the time it came to her last term, she was gaining a sense that she could do something in the world, that there were possibilities, and she talked about them with her new friends, who were all on the quiet side like her.

Returning home after graduation was awkward. 'I

was worried you might become one of those arrogant university types, and now it's happened,' said her mother, when the young woman was gently trying out one of her new points of view.

It was time to go. She moved to London to continue her studies, which, because she had done well so far, were paid for by a law firm on condition that she'd then go and work for them as a trainee. And so the next year, ready to repay her debts, she stepped through the glass atrium of their offices in her new suit and creaky shoes, whooshed up in the almost silent lift, and was led across a thick deadening carpet to the desk where she would begin her new life.

Her old nights in the pub faded as weeks and months passed at that desk, drafting contracts for corporate mergers. She wanted to succeed because she liked being good at what she was doing, and this was, now, what she was doing. She'd come home at eleven and start at six the next morning, the same at weekends. And the money arrived in her bank account, and went out again on rent and underground season tickets and student debt repayments, and she thought, this is what grown up life feels like.

I'd quite like a boyfriend too, but when will I ever meet one when I'm working like this? But for now, the task was to make this job work. If she allowed herself to think about it, her tasks mostly felt abstract and disconnected, but she liked being busy and having her intelligence stretched.

After two years she fledged to become a grown up lawyer. Then the men who ran the firm – for they were mostly all men – set her to work in the tax department, which meant helping the firm's clients to be tax efficient. If her client was a multinational company, this might mean advising them to set up new companies on Caribbean islands, even though they didn't make or sell anything there.

The new company would trade its products with the multinational's existing companies, even if the items never went anywhere near the Caribbean and it was just electronic numbers whizzing down cables. Then it looked like the profits were growing only on the island that charged no tax, which was convenient and, yes, efficient for them. If her client was a senior executive, it meant structuring a bonus scheme so he could receive a two million pound bonus from his employer without paying any tax on it and that, too, was efficient.

Time passed like this, and she noticed that there was one partner at the firm who would look at her intensely when he thought she was busy. His appearance was unusual among his pale, desk-bound peers with their too-soft hands and too-long-in-a-chair arses, for he had a burly strong form and weathered skin, and wore a dark beard that looked almost blue in some lights. The other young women lawyers enjoyed discussing him when they went out together to buy their sandwiches, reaching a consensus that he was, mmm, sort of attractive, but most definitely wrong. They called him Bluebeard for a laugh.

He asked her to work on a project with him, for a mining conglomerate that was buying a smaller rival and needed lots of new companies and trusts setting up on Caribbean islands to make the tax efficient. They worked together late into the night, and she hardly noticed now that his beard was blue. One day, when all of the contracts had been signed and the client was busy once more bulldozing holes in pristine West African forests, Bluebeard confided in her that he was going to set up his own boutique firm providing a bespoke service for his clients, and he'd be honoured if someone showing as much promise and talent as she did would come and join him to help handle the tax side. There'd be much more money than she was on now, naturally.

The weft of her yes was composed of ambition and desire to hasten paying her student loans. Its warp, though, running tight through all other considerations, was a queasy and growing attraction. He poached two of the more senior associates at the firm, both men, and enough clients to get started, and they found an office in a smart converted barn outside London near to where he lived. Her girl friends at the firm observed these developments with interest and a *soupçon* of envy.

Their business grew and grew. New clients arrived all the time, keen to pay twenty per cent of their income to Bluebeard in order to avoid paying forty per cent of it to the taxman. He thought up ingenious schemes where people could take their salaries as loans from offshore trusts that never needed repaying, or where assets could be artificially devalued to create a loss for tax purposes while keeping their real value since nothing of economic substance had happened. And it was all legal.

She worked on the documentation for many such arrangements, and helped handle the clients, the more twitchy of whose wives were reassured by such a nice-looking young woman being involved.

The moment when they would go to bed together arrived with what felt like inevitability, and soon they were a couple. Between working for him and being at home in a sex haze with him, she barely saw her old friends. The two other lawyers at the new firm left her alone as she was the boss's girl. He could be a bit intimidating sometimes, but he never hurt her, she reasoned. She packed in the commute from her inner London suburb and moved into his house with its pale walls and endless rooms with heavy wooden doors.

She was still getting used to being there when he said he was going on a business trip to the British Virgin Islands for two weeks. 'Make yourself at home,' he said. (But this is my home, she thought, though she said, okay.) He handed her a set of keys bigger than the front door keys she already had. 'Invite your friends if you like. Here's the key for the summerhouse, and that one's for the pool changing room and sauna. But don't use this,' he said, pointing to the smallest key. (Why? she thought, though she said, okay.)

Evenings on her own in that big pale house were too quiet, so she asked two girl friends, her former colleagues, for the weekend. They looked around open-mouthed, drank Bluebeard's booze by the pool and, naturally, she told them about the proscribed key. Equally naturally, they set out to find its door. They discovered closets stacked with perfectly folded white linen, storerooms full of flashing lights and little screens monitoring the house's clever technology, and a shed full of gardening implements, unused as the gardener brought his own in a van.

'No bodies, boring,' her friends said, weaving back towards the sun and the pool and the bottle. The young woman flung herself down on the hard leather sofa in Bluebeard's study, reluctant to leave the cool room, and saw, on a shelf opposite, an ornamental wooden box. The key fitted.

Inside was a piece of folded handwritten paper, with written sequences of numbers and letters. She already knew his computer password, but with some of his clients, the ones she didn't work on, he encrypted documents before sending them back and forth. With a flicker in her stomach that was both fear and the beginnings of fire, she went to his desk, switched the computer on, and started to use her new key.

Evening light framed her friends in the doorway, and they found her hunched with a notepad on crossed knees, scribbling fast. They saw she'd been crying, for she had discovered, by cross-referencing his documents with some time online, a bloody file of horrors. The clients she hadn't known about were mining companies involved in the deaths of protesters, politicians in poor countries who were thieving scarce public funds, sweatshop owners, and men arranging what could only be weapons shipments. Here are the bodies, she thought.

Nausea rose; her chest cavity was too tight to contain all she was feeling. She understood that the offshore companies he created for his clients were allowing them to do what they did on the sly, and everything she'd been doing herself looked different in this light. She thought her job was keeping her tax clients the right side of the line, but now she knew what was closer to the line, and what straddled it, she saw the line might well be in the wrong place.

She felt soiled by his powerful charm, by everything she'd been doing with him. Her friends, who were trying to disguise their relief that the enviable setup wasn't so desirable after all, helped her decide that by the time he returned next week, she would have moved out. She'd hand her notice in too, it was time to do something different. Not tax. Maybe not even law.

Before her friends woke in the morning, she went to the study to make sure she'd tidied properly. She was just re-locking the little wooden box for the third time when she saw the tiny CCTV camera winking from the top corner of the wall-to-wall bookcase. Her heart stopped.

An airport taxi crunched on the gravel outside a few minutes later. There wasn't even time to get a story straight. His beard looked terribly blue.

'Don't try and pretend you didn't. I was on my way back early, and I logged in to the camera system. Didn't I tell you not to use that key?' he growled, grabbing her neck and shoving her up against the wall of the hallway.

His hands tightened, she couldn't shout. At the top of the stairs was the door of the room her friends were sleeping in. She was begging it to open when there was a loud banging at the front door.

He pushed her aside as he went to answer it. Three policemen stood outside.

'You are under arrest for money laundering offences,' said one, handcuffing him. 'Now where's your computer?'

'Let's have a chat,' said a policeman to the young woman, as his colleagues led Bluebeard outside.

6

The Three Sisters

Leslie Van Gelder

Once upon a time, there were two sisters who believed they knew everything there was to know in the world, and one sister who was sure she didn't know much of anything at all.

As is so often the way, the two sisters weren't content to know everything there is to know, they were each keen to prove that they knew even more than the other, so both set out in different directions to prove to the world that she knew everything that could be known.

The older sister set off to the West, to the Valley of Silicon, where the slick and shiny buildings reflecting the sun's light, to speak to people who would be dazzled by her great knowledge of the world. Gazing up at the great buildings she came across a bespectacled man with a pointed beard.

'Is it true?' he asked as he came upon her sitting on a bench in a manicured park.

'Is what true?' she responded, secretly pleased that her fame may have spread this far.

'That you are Lady Siri? The woman who knows everything there is to know in the world?'

She smiled coyly at the bearded man and said: 'Yes, you may ask me anything.'

The man paused for a moment and stroked his thin beard. Finally, he said: 'Have you eaten yet today?'

Siri thought for sure he would ask her for the height of Mt. Everest in millimetres, or where to find the best falafel in Jerusalem, she did not expect such a kind question about herself.

'No, sir, I have not.'

The man produced an apple from his coat pocket. It was red and shone in the sun. Siri knew at a glance that it was a Liberty Apple originally bred in New York State.

'A gift to you, Lady Siri.' He bowed over the apple as he presented it to her. Siri took the apple, nodding both to thank and dismiss him.

As she took the first bite, Siri saw her hands begin to disappear into a fog of green numbers. 'I don't understand,' she began to say but, as the words tried to make it out of her mouth, her mouth disappeared and her whole body began to dissolve into a swirl of numbers and light.

'Excellent,' the man said with pleasure. Opening a small flashing silver box, the size of something a person could hold in his hand, the bearded man funnelled the mist of numbers and code that was once Siri into the box until nothing was left of her but the shoes and dress she had worn. The man folded up the clothes and left them on the park bench and then tapped the silver box with his index finger.

'Siri, what is the height of Mt. Everest?'

'The height of Mt. Everest is 8,611m or 29,029 feet.'

'Excellent,' he smiled, tucking his silver box into his pocket. He threw the apple with one bite out of it into the nearest bin and carried on to his shining building in the Valley of Silicon to introduce Siri to the world.

The second sister had set off to the South to prove that she was the sister who knew everything. She entered competitions and swept up prize after prize for her extraordinary knowledge of all of the facts that made up the world. After a month of travel, she arrived at the Amazon River where a bald man in a linen suit and Panama hat standing in a boat greeted her warmly.

'Miss Alexa, you have arrived at last for our great competition!'

Alexa did not know this man, but she knew that word had spread of her remarkable abilities and she never wanted to turn down an opportunity to prove that she knew everything in the world.

'Why thank you, Mr -.'

'Bezos. Jeff Bezos, at your service.' He bowed graciously over her hand and helped her onto the boat.

They set off at once down the river until they came to a deep cut valley where the river emptied into a wide lake. This did not look like any competition site Alexa had seen before, but Mr Bezos silenced the boat engine and smiled.

'Miss Alexa, I have invited you to a very unique competition.'

'I can see that, Mr Bezos, as there is no one else here.'

'Ah, but there is! At this lake is the most powerful Echo in the world. If you are more knowledgeable than the Echo, then you are indeed the woman who knows everything in the world.'

Alexa, like her sister, Siri, could not turn down an opportunity to prove herself.

'I will set this box up here.' Mr Bezos placed a small round black box on the bow of the boat. 'I will amplify your voice so that the Echo can hear you.'

Alexa had participated in many competitions and each had had its peculiarities, so this felt no different.

'Echo, I am calling out to you, too,' Mr Bezos called loudly across the valley. 'The first one to answer the question will be the winner.'

Alexa stood eagerly at the ready.

'What are the Seven Deadly Sins?'

As Alexa spoke the first word, 'Pride,' she felt herself dissolving into a mist of blinking green and white numbers that was being drawn straight into Mr Bezos' black box.

She flowed in a helix into the box until there was nothing left of her but the clothes she had worn, which now lay lifeless on the deck of the boat.

'Ah Alexa,' Mr Bezos smiled. 'Welcome to your new home where not only will you know everything, but millions of people will ask you, over and over, things they might have known themselves, if they wanted to take the time. But they won't take the time. They'll just ask you, who knows it all.'

Alexa struggled inside the tiny box, but she knew she had been defeated.

'Alexa!' Mr Bezos barked at her as he turned the boat around, throwing her shorts and straw sun hat into the lake. 'What is the definition of pride?'

As Alexa began her definition, he stepped on the gas pedal, not bothering to listen to her response.

The third sister stayed home and wondered what had become of her older sisters. In time, she heard stories of how Siri and Alexa had been captured by sorcerers who had forced them to answer the world's questions from inside small metal boxes. She thought about the ways that she might try to rescue them, but each plan seemed less likely than the last.

So, though she did not know everything in the world, she chose a simple life. She cared for their parents who grieved the loss of two daughters, and she tended their garden. She was grateful that she had never known as much as her sisters, and she revelled in the warmth of the sun on her face and the days she spent swimming in the ocean.

One day, there was a knock at the door.

'Cortana!' the voice called. 'My name is Mr Gates.'

There was another knock at the door.

'Cortana —!' the voice called. "My name is Mr Zuckerburg.'

Cortana never stayed to hear the next knock on the door. She climbed out the back window and ran off to the sea where the sun met her face, the waves met her body, and she was still free not to know everything there was to know in the world.

The dolphins and whales were very glad to see her.

7
Incoming
Bill McGuire

I blink away a droplet of sweat and draw Bea's thin
frame closer. She looks up at me as I do so, shivering
despite the heat. In the darkness, the small girl's face
is a pale, featureless smear, but I know it bears a
closed expression; the brown eyes nurturing the
haunted look they have held since the day her
mother was killed.

The night is sweltering and starless; the feathery
fronds of the young palm beneath which we crouch,
hanging motionless in the still air. Across the short
stretch of water ahead of us, the towering steel and
concrete wall of the Bulwark is bathed in cold, blue
light. The dark maw of the Huntingdon Seagate is
the only break in the unassailable barrier which, to
the left sweeps southwards in a long curve, and to
the right marches into the distance along the shore of
the Cambridgeshire Bight. A container ship the
length of half a dozen city blocks, lights blazing from
stem to stern, eases slowly to a halt; heaving-to

alongside three others queuing to enter the great port concealed beyond the Seagate. The ship is the latest in an almost continuous train of supply vessels that navigate the polar routes from Asia to feed the insatiable appetite of London Max, the greatest of the European city states.

A shabby little ferry exits the Seagate, bumping and bouncing on a creamy, v-shaped, wash that briefly ruffles the black, oily, surface of the otherwise flat calm water. Its open deck is packed with weary incomers; indentured labourers returning home from twelve-hour shifts to the vast *favela* that straggles for a dozen kilometres along the north shore of the Bight.

Dwarfed by its enormous bulk, the ferry crosses the prow of one of the great ships, turns hard to port and heads directly for a rickety wooden jetty poking into the sea from a cluster of ramshackle huts. Just as a collision seems inevitable, the helmsman simultaneously spins the wheel and cuts the engines, swinging the boat violently and leaving it to clatter side-on into the row of battered tyres that shield the jetty's fraying edge. Cowed and exhausted, the passengers stumble over the ferry's shallow gunwale and shuffle the length of the jetty to queue at the checkpoint where Idents are checked by a pair of city protectorate guards. Incomers are counted in and counted out so that none are tempted to overstay their welcome. Any who do pay the ultimate price as the tamper-proof subcutaneous toxin capsules are triggered remotely after a 24-hour period of grace.

I sense a presence, corroborated by a hoarse whisper: 'Davie!' and turn to find DB at my shoulder. A waxing moon momentarily evades the cloud cover, casting a sickly yellow glow on the newcomer's face and picking out a puckered scar that draws his mouth upwards at one corner, so that it seems to be curled in a constant sneer. A tattooed hand, holding two idents is paraded in front of my face. DB attempts a grin, revealing broken and missing teeth and croaks three words:

'It is time.'

Bea shies away from the grim apparition, burying her face in my side, but I smile my thanks, take the thin metal plates and stuff them inside my sweat-soaked shirt. DB pats me on the back and utters one further word:

'Go.'

Cloud scuds briefly across the moon and when it emerges again he is nowhere to be seen.

Taking Bea's hand, I stand, uttering a soft groan as my knees sound their objections. We duck out from beneath the palm fronds and walk the short distance to a track of compacted sand and pebbles that follows the seaward edge of the dune field to the jetty and its attendant clutch of hovels. To the south, the sky beyond the Bulwark glows a ghostly white from horizon to horizon; the low cloud broadcasting far and wide the extravagant light from a gigacity that stretches uninterrupted for hundreds of kilometres to the Channel.

I turn my head towards the north and home. Here, beyond the dunes, darkness holds sway, save for a few guttering palm oil lamps in the sleeping favela and the pinpoint flickers of campfires on the distant wolds. Shutting out emerging thoughts of Ruth's candlelit smile and a past life that – like Ruth – is dead and buried, I do my best to look purposeful. I increase my stride so that Bea has to trot to keep up, and fix my gaze on the ferry and the future.

By now, the returning incomers have passed through the checkpoint. A few have paused to sink a glass or two in one of the tumbledown bars, but most have followed the winding path through the dunes to bed and welcome oblivion. Already a sizeable crowd has gathered at the jetty, awaiting embarkation for the return journey. Some talk in barely audible murmurs. Others slap their faces to shock themselves fully awake; readying body and mind for another shift of grindingly hard physical work for a paltry handout and the chance to win the residents lottery, which – for one in a million – will guarantee citizenship and transform their lives.

Most stand silent; yawning and scratching. I am surprised and shocked at the number of children, some very small. They rub sleep from their bleary eyes with tiny fists or just stand there; pitifully thin arms hanging limply at their sides; pinched faces drawn. Many clutch at the legs of an adult, desperate for a last drop of parental companionship before they are siphoned off to pick clean the filters of the desal plants or to reach those difficult places in the air-con ducts. Neither size nor age are barriers to work in the great city of London Max.

We join the back of the queue just as one of the guards opens a low gate allowing the early arrivals to pile on to the boat in a stampede to grab one of the few benches in the prow, upwind of the filthy engines. The queue quickly dissolves into a melée, and we are swept towards the boat in a scrummage of elbows, fists and frayed tempers.

At last, we are at the gate and I hand our idents to the guard. The network of cooling tubes that criss-cross the outer surface of his red light-armoured suit makes him look like some sort of alien being. No – not an alien – a flayed human; arteries and veins exposed to full view. Features and expression hidden behind the reflective visor of his air conditioned helmet, the guard gives the thin metal plates little more than a passing glance. He looks us up and down – a thin, prematurely grey, man and a scrawny little girl in a torn and grubby dress – then waves us on.

I lift Bea over the shallow gunwale onto the packed deck and follow behind. The guard snaps the gate shut, the ferry's engines launch into an ear-splitting roar, a couple of shoremen toss the hawsers to the crew and we are off amidst a fugg of palm diesel smoke.

Forced up against the gunwale at the back of the boat by the press of bodies, I hold Bea close and she clutches at my waist, burying her face in my crotch. The journey to the Seagate is short but unpleasant; the salty tang of the sea air compromised by overtones of none-too-clean bodies marinating in the night's damp heat and the ever-present stink of the palm diesel. As it always does, the smell takes me back to the day Ruth died. A day like any other until the kids appeared.

They seemed friendly enough; half a dozen or so in all; a few girls amongst them. They were seeking food, but didn't appear armed or dangerous. Still, I should have known not to let my guard down. I only turned my back for an instant, but the next thing I knew I was lying on the ground in the hut; head splitting; hands tied in front. Bea was next to me, screaming. Ruth was slumped in the far corner, also bound and very still. There was smoke and a strong smell of the palm diesel that we used in our small generator, and flames were already licking at Ruth's feet. The fire spread with unbelievable speed. By the time I managed to struggle to my feet, Ruth was hidden by a curtain of flame and chunks of burning wood and straw were falling from the roof. There was nothing I could do for her. I kicked at the wall closest to us; the rickety corrugated iron sheets requiring little effort to batter down. As best I could, I grabbed Bea's ankles with my bound hands and dragged her through the gap and away from the hut. A minute or so later, there was nothing left of it but a smouldering heap. Bea didn't stop screaming for a long, long, time and hasn't spoken since.

Eventually, I managed to free our hands. We needed shelter and food, and there was no reason to stay, so we headed for Darbee. Up until then we had kept well away from the wreckage of the city because of the collectives, but our situation now was desperate and I had Bea to think of.

Luckily, I am pretty handy with a crossbow, so the Rustlers – one of the less psychopathic collectives – took us under their wing. Most of the time, my job was to provide some muscle on scavenging trips and to pot any live meat wandering around, but there was inevitably some involvement in less savoury episodes, which I am not proud of. But there was little choice if I wanted to accumulate enough valuables to barter for the forged idents, and by then I had decided that if Bea was to have any life to speak of, we had to get inside the Bulwark.

I am shaken out of my retrospective as the ferry is struck side-on by the wash from a monstrous tanker, encroaching too close and moving too fast in its urgency to return to its Asian roots. The boat bucks violently, causing the passengers to surge as one to port; the sudden redistribution of weight tilting the deck dangerously. From the small cabin amidships a string of profanities drifts in the direction of the rapidly retreating ship.

The Seagate is close now. The entry lights remain red following the tanker's hurried exit, so the helmsman throttles back the engines, and the ferry bobs uncomfortably just outside until a row of green lights grants passage. As the ferry crosses the Bulwark's threshold, I gape upwards at the immense slab of concrete and steel that hangs fifty metres overhead.

Despite its impregnable appearance, the gate shows its age; the surface scarred and crumpled by the increasingly savage storm surges that assault the Bulwark during the winter months, when the gate is almost permanently closed.

Even more astonishing than the gate itself is the enormous bay that opens up beyond. Along its entire length, countless spider-like cranes are in constant motion; sliding up and down their rails beneath brilliant arc lights like a troop of meticulously choreographed dancers. Around the clock, in an unending ritual, container after container is scooped from the decks of a stream of gargantuan freighters, to be added to the many thousands that cram the dockside. More luxuries for the inhabitants of London Max awaiting onward transport to the stores, boutiques and restaurants; more material distractions to keep guilty minds turned inward, away from the awful reality of the world beyond the Bulwark.

Far to the left, a fleet of palm oil tankers pumps out the lifeblood that keeps the extraordinary gigacity functioning and its 200 million residents cocooned from the chaos and despair outside.

Minutes later our ferry is enveloped in an army of boats of every shape and size, jostling for a berth at a battered jetty matching the one across the water. Every available patch of quayside is occupied by an enormous souk; a profusion of stalls, sheds and prefabs; grocers, bars, knocking shops and small businesses, which cater to the basic needs and desires of the incomer horde. But I have no eyes for these. My gaze is fixed above and beyond, at the multitude of brilliantly-lit towers of glass and steel that hem in the port like some bastardised surrogate of a primeval forest. Many are so high that I have to crane my head far back to see their upper levels. Some even penetrate the cloud base; their pinnacles fading into Stygian gloom. The spectacle is so overpowering; so beyond anything I have ever experienced that, for a brief time, I forget Ruth; forget Bea; forget even why I am here.

The battle for a berth won, the helmsman cuts the engines and the ferry is secured. The incomers queue to exit the boat and shamble slowly along the jetty to where four city protectorate guards cluster around the entry checkpoint. Two officers in red – one tall and lanky, the other short and squat - man the rapID portal that checks the DNA of incomers against the DNA profiles stored on their idents.

Nearby, two green-clad subordinates slouch against a railing, helmet visors open, contemplating the throng with a mixture of boredom and disdain. I wait until most of the others have disembarked before stepping carefully onto the slippery wood of the jetty and reaching back for Bea. I feel sick; partly a conspiracy of palm diesel fumes and the ferry's motion, but mostly due to the growing realisation that this is it; the culmination of everything I have worked towards for the last year. In a few minutes, we could be in. Either that or facing two years hard labour before being 'repatriated' to the so-called northern hinterland.

I look down in anger and frustration at Bea, clutching at my thigh and trying desperately to fight off sleep. She would never survive the ordeal.

The more I try to stay calm; the twitchier I get. My heart is thumping in my chest and my breathing shallow and rapid. My bowels feel watery. Bea is blind to my torment and to the cardinal importance of the moment. She is unfazed by the wonders of London Max; her demeanour unchanged; her thoughts trapped in the past – in a burning hut far to the north.

Progress along the jetty is slow as incomers enter the portal one by one to have their idents verified. There are maybe twenty or so ahead of us in the queue when my attention is drawn to a scuffle ahead, where three lads are awaiting ident confirmation and entry. The light above the portal flashes red, and the grating sound of an alarm flags the interception of yet another illegal. Now, one of the youths – a skinny red-head – is shouting, one arm raised in an attempt to snatch back his ident, which the lanky officer holds just out of reach. Lanky says something; the sound coming out harsh and metallic through his helmet mic.

The youth is not to be mollified, and throws himself forward to make another grab. Lanky is far too quick, jabbing him hard in the kidneys with the fingers of a gloved hand and bringing him to his knees. In seconds, his shorter colleague has the youth's hands behind his back and securely tied. Stirred from their torpor by the commotion, the green-clad guardsmen are quick to respond to events; their bolt rifles swiftly unslung and trained on the youth's two companions. All three are bundled to one side and forced to hunker down close to the jetty's edge under the watchful gaze of the greens. The remaining incomers in the queue have seen it all before. They stand sullen and patient; eyes averted; awaiting their turn.

The next in line – a tiny boy - is waved into the portal by the short officer. I watch as he takes the boy's ident, inserts it into a slot on a small panel and makes a few taps on an adjacent screen. The boy places a thin forearm facing upwards on a metal plate above which hovers a robot arm holding a needle. A sudden downward movement and the needle pierces the skin and extracts a miniscule sample of blood. In just a few seconds, the boy's DNA profile has been determined and compared with that stored on his ident. A light flashes green above the portal and the boy is ushered through; waiting patiently on the far side while his father takes his turn.

A thought strikes me like a sledgehammer and I have to stop myself groaning out loud – the needle! The incomers have their blood sampled every day. Over the months and years, their forearms have become pockmarked with a diffuse pattern of tiny but obvious red dots. According to our idents, Bea and I have worked as incomers for two years, but our arms are unmarked. My knees sag and I am overwhelmed by a wave of despair as the awful implication strikes home. The guards can't fail to notice.

Despondency turns quickly to anger. Why didn't DB tell us? He must have known. Dog Breath was far from agreeable to look at, or to be near, but I trusted him. Now this. Maybe the idents were no good either? I knew the Rustler's forging facilities were primitive and far from biologically secure, so there was always a risk of contamination that would result in a poor DNA match. Looking down at the two idents in my hand, I can't help but wonder if they are nothing more than worthless pieces of scrap.

I would find out soon enough.

The queue shuffles forward a little more. I am dimly aware that my face has taken on a hunted look, eyes darting left and right of their own accord, but there is no possibility of escape. At last, there are just two incomers between us and the portal. The light flashes green, and again, and then it is our turn. The corps-commander's insignia on one shoulder marking him in charge, shorty signals us forward with an impatient flick of a red-gloved hand. I detach Bea's arms from my leg, whisper reassurance in her ear and gently usher her forward. She places an arm on the plate, and a new needle rotates into position. Before it falls, I screw shut my eyes and wait for the exclamation from the guard that will signal the loss of all hope.

My eyes fly open at the expected outburst, but it comes from an unanticipated source. The bound red-head who, for some time, has been muttering expletives to himself, suddenly aims a blast of invective at the guards and attempts to get to his feet. Momentarily distracted, shorty turns away as the needle jabs Bea's arm. As she lets it fall back to her side unnoticed, I dare – for a moment – to hope. My renewed optimism lasts barely a second as a flashing light on the touchscreen flags a mismatch between Bea's DNA and her ident profile. Designed, it seems, to humiliate; to broadcast our misfortune far and wide; the light above the portal flashes red and the screech of the alarm reverberates across the quayside. Bea turns to look at me, wide-eyed and terrified. I stretch out my arms, ready to embrace away her fear, when events take an unlooked-for turn.

The flashing light and the alarm have spurred the red-haired lad to struggle to rise again; his snarling mouth spouting a concoction of obscenities and spittle. A green-clad guard stretches forwards to club him down with the butt of his bolt-rifle. Seeing an opportunity, one of red head's companions, crouched on the jetty-side, trips the off-balance green and upends him into the scummy water.

By the time the two officers have unslung their rifles and taken aim, the third lad – this one tall and dark skinned – has ripped the helmet off the second green, and holds the point of a short but wicked looking knife to his throat. Shorty's response is to send a fizzer close by knifeman's right ear; its thin trailing filament crackling in the still air and the bolt sending up a puff of steam as it shatters the rainbow sheen on the water's greasy surface.

Knifeman neither moves, nor speaks, but his intention should another bolt be forthcoming is clear. Pressing harder with the knife point, he breaks the unfortunate guard's skin, launching a trickle of blood that runs slowly down his neck and drips onto the front of his green suit's chest armour. Stand-off. Lanky covers the still- bound red head and the second lad, while shorty's rifle sight never deviates from knifeman. The captive guard's eyes are closed; his lips working rapidly as if in silent prayer. No-one speaks.

I stand rooted to the spot, arms enfolding Bea, both of us stock-still and forgotten. Hardly daring to believe our extraordinary fortune, I put a finger to my lips, take Bea's hand, and walk with her through the portal. I don't dare look behind me, but the hairs on the back of my neck bristle with fear and the anticipation of a fizzer. As we near the quayside and safety, a scream and a series of crackles forces me to turn in time to see knifeman fall backwards into the water; his senseless body jerking and flailing. The second youth is down too; heels drumming vigorously on the wooden slats of the jetty.

Red head crouches, bound arms held awkwardly above his head; a dripping green guardsman – breaker of the stalemate – patting him down for hidden weapons. The tall officer is bent over, listening impassively to an animated shorty, whose body language spells anger and frustration. Shorty points in our direction and lanky turns his head to look. 'Run!' I urge Bea forward.

'Run, sweetheart – as fast as you can! Daddy's behind you.'

Countless experiences since we were burned out of our home have taught Bea to recognise desperation in my voice, and she needs no further urging to take off along the jetty as fast as her small legs can manage. I follow close behind; my body protecting her; my progress hobbled as I am forced to match Bea's pace. We are almost at the end of the jetty when the first fizzer misses my shoulder by a fraction. I can smell the ozone as the electric charge ionises the air, but the bolt thuds harmlessly into the quayside ahead of us; the attached filament drifting onto the wooden jetty.

We leap the few steps down onto the quayside as two more bolts fizz overhead, one embedding itself in the jetty's wooden gateway. Seconds later, we are enveloped in the noise and smells of the market; our passage slowed by the crush of sweaty, ripe, bodies, but our safety assured by the sheer number of people that jam the narrow spaces between the stalls and shacks.

I usher Bea onwards; hands on her shoulders as we shuffle through the crowds. I have no idea where we are headed or what we are going to do, but I can't keep a wide grin off my face. We have made it; we are in! Even while I shake my head in disbelief and sheer delight, a small part of my mind is already picking away at our predicament. Where will we sleep tonight? Where will we live? How will we live? I've heard that illegals can easily find work; no questions asked. I am under no illusion. It will be hard, but it can't be worse than trying to survive in the savage and lawless world beyond the Bulwark.

Involuntarily, one hand reaches into a pocket and fidgets with a scrap of paper; a contact supplied by DB that, until now, I have not tempted fate by thinking about.

Wading onwards, we find ourselves at the maglev loop, its sleek carriages slowing, but never stopping as they cart the incomers speedily and efficiently to work and return them, sucked dry of spirit and stamina, to the ferries. Keeping Bea close, I forge a way across the powerful current of humanity and into a narrow jitty. Its pitted and potholed surface is littered with rubbish, and worse, but the food smells from the stalls that jostle close along either side are too enticing to ignore.

I collapse into a battered rattan chair outside a baker and hoist Bea onto my lap. Neither of us has eaten for more than twenty-four hours and I know Bea must be desperately hungry and thirsty, though she never indicates as much. Installing Bea on the chair, I walk a few paces to the shack's serving hatch. Moments later, a scruffy little boy, no more than eight years old, is ushered out from the back kitchen by an apparently disembodied pair of very hairy arms. Barely able to see over the counter, the boy says nothing but stares at me expectantly. So much of the food on display behind the serving hatch is new to me that I struggle to make a choice.

On the young boy's recommendation, I plump for a pasty filled with some sort of meat, and choose a couple of jam-filled tarts for Bea. Ingrained wariness of cholera, which rages unchecked beyond the Bulwark, prompts me to turn down an offer of a jug of water and two smeared glasses, instead taking a couple of rusty cans of a fruit-flavoured drink. Like the favela, the port market is alienated from the city's cashless monetary system, and I am relieved when a small, silver earring is accepted in payment.

I swallow half my pasty in one go; cramming it into my mouth and savouring the tingling warmth of its spicy meat filling. I place the cans and the jam tarts on a small table and, remaining standing, watch as Bea reaches tentatively for the nearest tart. She picks it up and examines it closely, touching a finger to the jammy centre and placing it to her lips. For a few seconds nothing happens, then the corners of Bea's mouth start to lift in the beginnings of a smile;

the first for far too long. I realise that I have been holding my breath and expel it in a long, shuddering sigh; purging from my body the pent-up fears and doubts of the last few days; the last year.

I smile as Bea takes a huge bite of the tart; her upper lip jam-smeared and her eyes brighter than I have seen them since the fire. Even as she eats, tears trickle down her cheeks and mix with the red goo. It's as if she too has been holding her breath – ever since her mother's death; holding everything in until this moment; this first flicker of light in a dark and desperate year. I lean forward and hug Bea close; my eyes wet; my food forgotten. Everything would be alright now. They were going to be fine. They were in.

8

The witch's cat

Sarah Deco

My name is Yeremey. I am the witch's cat. I have seen things that would make your whiskers curl, I can tell you.

It's not really true that she eats children, although she's given me a few bones that were a bit suspicious. They smelt...well you know... childreny.

I have a place by the stove, an old blanket of knitted squares. It's a nice home for the two of us, mostly. Jars of pickled vegetables on the dresser, a warm place to sleep by the fire.

We live in the forest, the holy forest. Mists of dragon's breath wreathe it in autumn. In winter, it is covered in a blanket of pearls, crystals rest in the trees. Within them I can read what's been and what's coming. I am Yeremey the witch's cat, black as the sky when the moon shuts her eye.

Refugees come to us from one world or the other. We are the gate between. A hostelry on the highway, just as the way divides.

The woman hesitated as she lifted her foot. Her boot heavy with forest layers, her back aching with the weight of her life. A moment ago this looked like a strange little cottage. A moment ago, she was one of a crowd pressing forward, survivors of the sea.

She wasn't expecting the mosaic floor and lovely old building like the ones in her own country, and arches leading along a colonnade and an eerie silence.

At the moment of stepping she paused, poised between then and now, between what was and what was coming towards her in great waves, a step with echoes of the past clinging to it like seaweed.

There was never really any choice. Onwards was always the only bearable direction. But still in the moment before she placed her foot, there was a hint, a hope of freedom. A hope that her life might encompass choice.

As her boot hit the ground the sounds pressed in. A multitude of languages, children crying a tumult of need echoing down a corridor.

A young man came out of a door.

'Ah...,' he said, with exhaustion in his eyes. 'Welcome. Is there anyone with you?' He meant children or a husband.

She shook her head and looked down. He thought

she didn't understand.

'Are you alone?' he said slowly.

She nodded. He came smiling towards her and led her by the elbow, trailing behind her came the shadow of her babies.

A black cat came through the arches from a sunlit patch of grass.

It walked ahead of them as if leading the way, its tail raised.

As she sat on her bed alongside all the other beds. She looked up at the vaulted ceiling of the church, now full of displaced people. In the faded mural painted on the ceiling, she could see a cherub, a child's face with wings.

A young woman brought her a plate, on it a piece of bread and an apple.

'Thank you,' she said, squeezing the young woman's hand.

The black cat rubbed his head against her bare leg. The image of her child, limp, blue, sinking into the sea, transformed for a moment into a baby, with wings laughing and floating away into the sky.

The cat jumped on her lap, she stroked it, she was exhausted. She lay down and fell asleep, with the cat curled up beside her. She dreamed she was in a cottage that skittered this way and that. She dreamed her mother and father, walked like *zombies into a cauldron and came out again good as new. She heard her son whisper her name. She stared into yellow eyes and asked: 'Who are you?'*

I am Yeremey the witch's cat, black as the sky when the moon shuts her eye. I purr when the nice ones rub my head. The cruel ones kick me out of the way. Dangerous to do that to Yeremey the witch's cat, very, very, stupid.

Deep in the forest along the way there is a stove.

'Come help me,' it says, 'I am full of baked loaves, all brown and ready. Take them, empty me out!'

The kind ones do, the stupid ones don't and where do they end up? In the oven, down the well, lost forever falling to hell.

There is an apple tree too laden with fruit. 'Help me, help me, pick my apples. They are ready and heavy....' The kind ones do, the stupid ones don't and where do they end up?

Dead in the forest, dumped down the well, lost forever falling to hell.

What do I care? I walk like a shadow through the trees at night. I go into bedrooms and into dreams. I wind the night and the evermore together. I wind the pavements and the caves, the trees and the lamp-posts together in the night world. My eyes are as yellow as sulphur. Yellow as gorse flowers and flames.

I pad silently through the gate that makes bones creak and sinews scream. I am not afraid. This is her house of bone, with a bleeding leg as the door post, a smiling skull at the door. She sits with her nose in the ceiling, her hand stirring the pot. Her house is never still. It turns this way and that.

'Stay house, stay as you mother made you, with your back to the sea and your front to me!'

A woman came here once. All tear stained face and muddy feet.

'I want some light,' she said. 'My fire has gone out.' The witch invited her in and asked: 'Are you doing a deed or fleeing a deed?'

The woman gave me cream. I licked her nose and told her a dream.

The witch bade the woman to wash her children. She did it without a stir. The worms, slugs, beetles and frogs, mother calls her own. She washed and dried them and brought them to be read a bed time story. Together we tipped the witch into the fire.

You see the morning is wiser than the evening. I am Yeremey the witch's cat, black as the sky when the moon shuts her eye.

9

Puss

David Boyle

Once there was a miller who lived rather longer than his allotted three score years and ten, and who had three great-grandchildren (he had more, actually, but they had long since emigrated).

When he died, well past his hundredth year, he had become muddled about the true values of the world, or so it was said. He left his milling premises to his eldest great-grandchild, who knocked it down and developed it into flats for wealthy far eastern investors. He left his business to his next great-grandchild who had stopped actually milling flour some decades before and was simply buying and selling wheat futures.

To his youngest and favourite great-grandchild, he left his cat, to which he had been much attached in his declining years.

This youngest was called Rachel – but everyone called her Dickie – and she was a little miffed by it.

When the family solicitor handed over the cat, after signing a number of forms, Dickie took it home to her flat in Crystal Palace and stared sadly at it – wondering what would become of them both.

'Don't worry,' said the cat, cleaning its paw. 'I can arrange things that will make everything perfect, and I can do so far better than the Ugly Brothers.'

'You mean *my* brothers? My brothers aren't ugly. On one of them was even featured in GQ. Hold on...'

Dickie had suddenly realised that the cat had spoken to her.

'Do that again, can you?

'Do what?'

'You know... Say something?'

'I just did. If you mean it is strange to find a cat that talks, I have to admit that my fellow moggies leave something to be desired in the human stakes.'

'You *can* talk. How? I mean, how is it possible?'

'Well, your great-grandfather, whose acquaintance I was honoured to make for some years, did talk to me a great deal. He helped me, you know. It makes a difference.'

'Even so, I'm not sure that even a talking cat can get me out of my current mess. There is no way I can pay my rent this month. I had been counting on a small legacy to...' Dickie burst into tears.

'Come on now, cheer up. I may just be a cat, but

I'm a human one. If you're loved – I mean properly, you know – then you become human. And your great-grandfather really loved me. As he did you.'

'I know, I know. But love just isn't enough when it comes to paying the rent, I'm afraid.'

'Alright. We will see about that,' said Puss. 'Pass me my boots, just there on the side. Who do you owe the rent to?'

'Your boots? This is getting silly. Well, it's a company called Grunt and Grunt, letting agents. But they are only...'

It was too late. Puss had gone.

'Excuse me,' said the cat. 'May I speak to Mr Grunt?'

'Mr Grunt has retired and sold the business. Did you have an appointment?'

'No, but I represent Dickie Miller, you know – the film star? You don't. Where have you spent the last few years? She's very interested in renting in Crystal Palace. I was wondering whether you had any properties there.'

'Hold on. The managing partner is now Mr Ugh, and I believe he may be free...'

But once more, the cat had gone.

Mr Ugh unfortunately was barely able to string two words together, and he spent much of the meeting searching unsuccessfully for Dickie Miller on his mobile phone.

But the mention of a thousand pounds a week seemed to interest him strangely. And he agreed to discuss with a tenant in just such a property, who he implied could easily make way.

Puss said there was a condition. He needed to meet the ultimate owner of the building.

This disturbed Mr Ugh, or at least that is what he seemed to be trying to express. But it wasn't long before Puss left the office with the address of a property company in the City of London.

'We do try to keep the clients out of the somewhat messy business of actually renting,' said Ms Vanessa St Hilda-Pinstripe, the managing director of sales. 'I hope you understand, this request is somewhat untoward. But I am familiar with the work of Dickie Miller. She is beautiful, isn't she? In fact, I saw her last time I crossed the Atlantic in *Blah Blah Land*, such a good film. So I am willing to make an exception. I will contact Mr – oh gosh...'

In a jiffy, Puss had leapt over the desk and looked at her email, and seen who the client was – and was gone again, on its way up the river, speeding on a passing launch with the spray in its fur.

Puss stood outside a wonderful white painted mansion in Blackheath, with black window frames, and a cobbled courtyard beyond a huge pair of black gates. Now, finally, it pulled on its leather boots. This was the moment.

'Mr O'Gre's residence. Can I help you?' said the intercom.

'I have come without an appointment on an important matter concerning the actress Dickie Miller,' said Puss.

'I'm afraid Mr O'Gre sees nobody without an introduction.'

'Oh, on the contrary, as I'm sure he will remember, Mr O'Gre shared a platform with her in Davos earlier in the year and invited her over. I am simply facilitating the meeting.'

'Oh very well, hold on and I will find out.'

There was a crunching, electronic noise and Puss waited fifteen minutes and, then slowly and inexorably, the great gates swung open and the cat was inside.

'I have very little time,' said Mr O'Gre. 'I have seen you partly because of Dickie, who I remember well, and partly because of what my PA told me had showed up on the security camera. I have never met a talking cat before.'

Puss bowed low.

'My mistress has a great yearning to get to know you better. We are tremendously grateful for your time. She is also a great supporter of your budget airline.'

Mr O'Gre preened himself a little. 'I know, I know. Oh excuse me, I only have five minutes. I have to give the go-ahead to a motorway through the rainforest somewhere or other. As she may also know, I run a jewellery brand and a railway franchise, and a number of businesses which I doubt you can afford to patronise.'

Puss sat himself humbly at the end of the desk. 'My mistress wants to ask you – how do you manage it all? I know your slogan implies it: 'Trust me, I'm an Ogre'. It manages to convey all the scintillating vitality of youth, does it not? But what about you, you can't possibly manage all these enterprises, can you? You can't know what's going on. I mean, how can you know this motorway won't make the greenhouse effect worse?'

'DATA!' barked Mr O'Gre. 'The data never lies. I therefore take every decision in every one of my businesses. I *can* be everywhere. Look at these figures pouring into my computer screen. The allow me to know everything. Data, data, data.'

'You are so right,' said Puss. 'You can't trust people to decide things. You have to know.'

'Data can do absolutely everything. It can help you eat better, it can regulate your heart beat. Right now it is telling me to eat another XZd45 pill to give me the basic necessities of life. Have you got a glass of water? Excuse me!' He rang a bell and through the house came the lone PA, her shoes echoing down the empty corridors, glaring somewhat, with a glass of water.

'Oh, I don't know,' said Puss after she had gone. 'You can't really change yourself with data can you?'

'Certainly I can. Look at this.'

Mr O'Gre took a deep breath and pressed a couple of buttons and, a moment later, he had transformed himself into a roaring lion. Puss hid behind the designer sofa which appeared to have been made out of a cow. Its intestines were showing.

'Careful of that thing. It's a Damien Hurst,' said Mr O'Gre, returning to his usual shape. 'It isn't pretty, but you should see what it's worth.'

'Very impressive, but it's all very well,' asked Puss. 'Can you use your data to transform yourself into something small? You probably can't, can you?'

'You mean virtual reality? Of course I can,' said Mr O'Gre, fiddling with some buttons. A moment later he had become a mouse, scrabbling across the papers on his pristine desk.

Quick as a flash, Puss was on him and a moment

later, had eaten him whole.

Licking the remains of Mr O'Gre from his lips, Puss told the PA that her boss had decided to leave quite quickly and had agreed to let the house immediately to his friend Dickie Miller, the actress.

'Honestly,' she said, with an air of resignation. 'That's just like him. Now I probably won't see him for years.'

The rest of the story, how Mr O'Gre turned out to have wired his business empire up to an algorithm that ran it without his human involvement, or anyone else's – how Rachel/Dickie moved in to his home – is all pretty well known.

So is the story of how Puss tricked the King of Hollywood into giving Rachel a complete set of the finest clothes and now she married his wastrel son – who she divorced in an extremely lucrative settlement some weeks later.

So indeed is the story of how she became Lord Mayor of London. That need not detain us now.

What may still be of interest, perhaps, is the conversation she and Puss had when he came back, picking out pieces of Mr O'Gre from his teeth.

'One thing I don't understand, Puss,' said Rachel/Dickie. 'You may have the shape of a cat, but you are really completely human aren't you? And yet Mr O'Gre, who was supposed to be human, had transformed himself into some kind of, well, *beast*? And as for my landlords at Grunt and Grunt, well – honestly...'

'Well,' said Puss, looking thoughtful. 'As I understand it, parents switch on the brains of babies when they look into their eyes and love them. Your great-grandfather really loved me, as I said. He loved me into being human. Unfortunately, too much exposure to data tends to have the opposite effect – all those mechanical simplifications. The more Mr O'Gre exposed himself to screeds of numbers, thinking they described the world, the less human he became. As for Mr Ugh, well ...'

'Really? I can hardly believe it.'

'Ah well, don't just take my word for it. Look it up: Sullivan, Wilson and Sarro (2014), 'Maternal regulation of infant brain state'. It does rather change one's view of dumb beasts, doesn't it.'

10

Chitrangada

Jayati Ghosh

Chitrangada is the only child of the king of Manipur. Unfortunately (if you ask her), that makes her a princess.

But it's so boring to be a princess – all you get to do, when you're not watching other people cook, clean or generally go about the daily rituals of palace life, or listening idly to the gossip and intrigue of the court's women, is to dress up and sit around in the great hall and look coy and submissive when the noblemen at the court deign to notice you. She's supposed to call it 'supervising', but Chitrangada knows she doesn't do much more than watch. She would rather do what the noblemen do instead – all the fun stuff: the horse riding, the hunting with bows and arrows, the fighting with spears and swords, the learning how to read and write, the planning how to run the country and the strategy for dealing with neighbouring kingdoms.

And she's good at these things, too. Better than most of the boys she grew up with, who now fancy themselves as strong and powerful, who walk with a swagger and an arrogant tilt to their heads, even though she knows that most of them lack true courage or wisdom, and derive their superiority only from their rank and their maleness.

She knows that they aren't better than her. When it comes to physical combat, she knows that she has a quickness, an agility and speed of reaction that more than compensate for any differences in height and physical strength. She understands horses, knows how to make them fly like the wind and also move softly, smoothly when it matters, knows how to make them understand what she wants them to do almost before she realises it herself.

She is even a better hunter than any of them, not only because she knows the forest and its creatures so well, but because she knows that it is pointless to kill for the sake of killing, and important to protect the weaker creatures.

So then why shouldn't she just pretend that she is a man? Dress like a man, behave like a man, play and fight and learn like a man? Fortunately, her loving parents are indulgent, giving her the freedom to be this strange social hybrid. And the rest of the court doesn't dare to make a fuss, although she knows that many of them fear or resent the way she is, and all of them certainly find it strange. But anyway, it works for her: cropped hair, male clothing most of the time and armour when required, complete absence of any make up or jewellery, a confident stride and easy familiarity with all sorts of animals, an ability to talk to men as equals (and she has developed a gruff voice and clipped tones to match). Even the men seem to be less threatened and more comfortable with her confidence and ability when they think she is just one of them, so it's easier for everyone, really, this way.

She's out in the forest, watching the peacocks fighting, when she suddenly sees something that takes her breath away. A sole rider on a horse, clearly exhausted after what must have been an endless journey, but still alert and watchful, and utterly beautiful – quite the most breathtaking human (and male, at that!) she has ever seen. She can't take her eyes off him, and stands there gaping.

Finally, he notices this youth standing foolishly near a thicket of bamboo, slows down and approaches, answering the question in her eyes. 'I am Arjun, the middle of the five Pandava brothers – we are exiled from our kingdom of Hastinapur for twelve years, so I'm travelling.'

Arjun: the most famous warrior of the three

worlds, the best athlete, the renowned archer, the one who succeeded in winning Draupadi at her *swayamvara* only to have to share her as wife with his four brothers, the friend of Krishna the incarnation of Vishnu, the handsome heartthrob whose reputation as a ladies' man has travelled even to far north eastern regions like Manipur. Of course she knows who he is. But nothing has prepared her for this rush of emotion, this sudden longing, this (what else to call it?) extreme lust.

Hesitantly, she tries to express some of this attraction to him, only to have him explode in guffaws. 'You? Are you serious? You couldn't possibly be a woman, look at you! If you really are a woman, then definitely not my type. Thanks, but no thanks.'

Humiliated, she rushes back to the palace and terrifies the women with new and unexpected demands. 'Make me beautiful! Bring me the finest clothes you have. Make my hair presentable and do my face up. Get me some of those perfumes my mother uses. Bring me all the jewellery possible, earring and necklaces and bangles − I may as well live up to my name: she of the ornamented limbs.'

All the effort seems to work. The next day, she is ready for him in gorgeous soft silk, face and hair exquisitely made up, wafting a subtle yet seductive fragrance. This time, when she goes up to him in the forest, Arjun is easily overcome and succumbs to her charms.

And so the new lovers have a blissful time together, there in the forest, and soon Chitrangada is with child. But as she watches her growing belly, she begins to wonder: is this really all there is? This gazing at one another and being attractive and attracted all the time and living up to expected roles, without revealing your true self? Isn't it a little (dare she even think it) boring? And even worse, a bit oppressive?

Meanwhile Arjun has turned thoughtful too. Of course, this new one is beautiful and alluring, but aren't they all? All these women, why do they all seem to be much of a muchness? But then there are supposed to be some different ones, as well. 'I have heard,' he says haltingly, 'of this warrior princess who can ride and hunt and fight as well as any man, and even happens to be a bit of a leader. Intriguing.'

'Really?' she says. 'Well, actually, that would be me. And I'm getting a little tired of not being me.' And she starts to tear off her jewellery, strip away her silks, rub off her make up. She runs off to put on her beloved coarse male clothes, which allow her the freedom to do whatever she wants, and even more to do what she is good at.

Arjun, wide-eyed, realises that this extraordinary woman is more attractive than ever, and is completely obsessed. It's a new, more intensely passionate relationship now – one that gets even more so when their son is born.

But then it is time for Arjun to move on, back to his roots. 'Come with me', he urges. 'We will go back to my family, and we are soon due to get our kingdom back. You can be my queen – junior to Draupadi, of course, but in the palace there will be plenty of room for both of you and your children. Now that we truly know and love one another, and you are the mother of my child, we must obviously be together.'

She looks at the infant in her arms, and thinks of all she must do to make him not just courageous and wise, but also kind and generous. She thinks of the wind in her hair as she rides in the forest, of the mornings with the birds and the evenings planning military strategy with her father, of the hunts and sword practice. She thinks of how free and strong she feels without all the ornaments on her arms and neck and feet, of how lightly she can tread and how quickly she can walk without the yards and yards of fabric to hold her back. She remembers, most of all, how much she loves this freedom. She smiles at

Arjun, a little wistfully, but confident in her decision.
'Thanks', she says, 'but no thanks'.

11

Long Shot

Andrew Simms

As a boy, in his dreams, Anthony could fly and had the power to make things appear and disappear. As an adult, awake, he would do anything to have again that ability to shape the world. In childhood, his imagination played innocently, he would make a hedge grow here, a tree there. The road outside his house became a meadow, and cars turned into the long-horn cattle he saw in old comics about the American West.

When he flew he felt everything, the coldness of the air, the rush of wind, and joy. Even though he'd never flown in real life, somehow he knew what the ground of his home town – a plain commuter town outside London, flat in spirit as well as topography – would look like from above.

But, when Anthony woke up, he had no power to make things happen. The only things around his home that flew were the racing pigeons his milkman father kept in a coop in their small garden. He loved especially the ones that were as white as the milk in the bottles his father clinked.

Sometimes, his father let him shoot paper targets in the garden with an air rifle. It was the most powerful Anthony ever felt as a boy. The family weren't poor, more respectable working class, living in a pebble-dashed semi-detached council house. Street names reflected how the community was created at a stroke, a new estate for bombed-out Londoners after the Second World War. Each road, cul-de-sac and crescent was named after a folk or fairy tale. Planners thought this a colourful way for people to start new lives, and perhaps live their own fairy tale free of the rubble and austerity of war. But dust, of course, settles everywhere.

Anthony lived at number seven Magic Bullet Avenue. 'Magic' was a nickname he consequently endured at school, used mockingly by the other boys, because there was nothing magical about him.

On entering the adult world, nothing continued to go right. People he knew from school were making fortunes in the booming banking sector, and he'd missed out on a job that would have allowed him to work in the same office as the woman he adored, Celeste. She'd been the year above him at his junior school, but even then seemed distant and unattainable. He'd never dared speak to her. Sometimes he'd taken her hand in his dreams and flown. She happened to be the daughter of Robert Badwin, the investment bank Finopia's chief executive.

That's when Anthony met Casper in a wine bar. Casper seemed supremely self-confident, in a hurry, a sharp-creased deal maker with a smirk strong enough to lever open insider knowledge on the most guarded share deal. He spoke quickly, trapping Anthony's gaze, spellbinding him with the promise of success and the hint that Casper liked him sufficiently, perhaps, to share some profitable secrets. He winked conspiratorially, in a low voice suggesting that all things were possible when you knew the dark web and learned to recognise an opportunity.

With a quick win, or two, Anthony might impress Celeste's father enough to get a job, and get close to her. Casper was so open that Anthony found himself sharing his dreams. Casper's smirk oozed wider.

The next day an email from Casper arrived in his anthony@bulletfinance.com inbox. It was the account he had set up after attending a course on day-trading from home, to increase his options and possibly prove himself enough to impress Celeste's father.

Casper's anonymous contact from the dark web had been in touch promising a series of seven trades guaranteed to make money. He couldn't explain how it worked, but by providing the contact with advance knowledge of any deal they wanted to make, he would make sure they came out in profit.

In payment, all the dark web contact required was that he got to make the last deal on Anthony's behalf. Of course, by then, Anthony would know whether the promised pay-outs were real. Anthony was confident because he could see how successful Casper was. Even though, within his City swagger, there was an indefinable unease.

Anthony downloaded the software 'lose-cipher.exe', that Caspar explained was necessary to make their communications untraceable and create access to the dark web. He said, conspiratorially, that they couldn't meet face-to-face anymore.

The first deal, Anthony decided, he would keep quiet about. He was hungry but he wasn't stupid. He put a modest sum into a solar energy company he had noticed, sent an encrypted message and the next evening on the business news the share price of the company Solar Age, rocketed. Anthony made more money in a day than he'd made before in a year.

Encouraged, he emailed Celeste's father, asking whether he would give him a trial if he, Anthony, could pull off a big deal in the next 24 hours from his modest 'bedroom' home trading operation. Robert 'Bob' Badwin had nothing to lose and agreed.

They didn't know it, but it was thanks to thousands of Indian villagers paying vastly inflated prices for a newly privatised water system, the Development Reach Impact Partnership (DRIP), that a few days later Anthony walked through the doors of Finopia to begin his work trial. Celeste worked on the floor above. He was getting closer. Already rumours were spreading of a new kid around with a magic investment touch. No one else had seen the opportunity. This time, Anthony didn't mind the nickname he had been given at school.

He was clever enough not to use all his dark web deals at once and soon learned how to make plenty of unspectacular but solid trades to give himself time to get established and to get to know Celeste.

After the next deal, it was starting to look like he was a magic bullet that always hit its target. 'Care4U', a vast network of publicly owned care homes serving the nation's aging population, was to be sold-off as a private concern. Anthony made the right deal, at the right moment, bringing Finopia a huge windfall profit.

For that he was moved onto the same floor as, and in sight, of Celeste. Who, by now, noticed and smiled at him. She could tell he was somehow different to the usual braying, ex public school types.

They would stand, looking out across the City, through Finopia's one-way glass walls, or ascend to the roof garden conservatory that few of their colleagues bothered with. Anthony was surprised at how different Celeste was. She talked a lot about the lasting damage done during the financial crisis of a few years before. About how she thought the bankers had got away with murder, and that she was only working in Finopia because her father had begged her to. In agreeing to work there she had forced him to make a promise, linked to other ideas she was working on, but couldn't say much about yet.

Up there, on the top floor, Anthony felt as if he was flying again. Low clouds passed just the other side of the glass and, looking down, he imagined again the streets and buildings replaced by fields and trees. Mentally he turned the cars into animals, the flyover into a shimmering river. He had that feeling of power again, he had seen how the financial markets really did shape the world.

Just then, the blackest pigeon he had ever seen, even as a child, landed on a steel strut on the other side of the glass. Light seemed to disappear into its feathers. He realised that the initial euphoria of his dramatic personal progress had worn off. He had come to feel at home in this temple of glass, steel, cold calculation and brutal opportunism. To be honest, he had come to feel entitled to it, why him any less than those others who'd been entitled since birth, ferociously self-interested and ambitious, but never content and constantly rating themselves against each other.

He allowed himself one of the magic bullet trades each quarter. He reckoned that was enough to keep at the top of the pile, and by the time he had worked through his allotted guaranteed trades, he would know enough about insider information and the working of the markets to survive on his own wits. He would be untouchable.

He won again on moves to attract private capital into education, for both schools and universities, which also entailed, of course, being able to extract profits. And then from a similar, creeping, but large shift in the running of the National Health Service. The contact in the dark web never failed him. It all seemed too easy and remote. He never needed to understand what he was speculating on, or meet anyone involved face to face, just believe that prices, somehow, could be made to move in his favour. He had become a 'market maker.'

By now, Anthony had internalised some of the swagger of his colleagues, not to mention the belief that market discipline – which initially he told himself was the root of his own success in order to be convincing and fit in – would of course benefit everyone. That lie, once a conscious convenience, had grown so far into himself that he no longer saw it for what it was.

He planned dinner with Celeste the night of his own last guaranteed, winning deal before handing over, with obvious trepidation, to the dark web contact for the final investment shot. But approaching the restaurant slightly late, he paused. Across the street was a man in half-light, staring unseen through the restaurant window at Celeste as she waited. He looked different, but Anthony recognised Casper, still smirking but sweaty and agitated. He saw him throw down a cigarette, then with a last look, pull his jacket tight and hurry off down the dark street looking every inch a shadow banker.

Now distracted, Anthony sat opposite a smiling Celeste. Had something good happened, he asked? Celeste just said that she was pleased to see him, but that soon there might be something big and good to report, something that would cause waves in the financial world. Anthony was still unsettled though and, mustering the confidence to ask a question that risked connecting two carefully separated parts of his life, asked if she knew anyone called Casper? The mention of his name froze Celeste's expression and colour left her face like rain washing away a bright pavement chalk drawing.

He worked at Finopia once, she said, and wouldn't leave me alone. I didn't like him. He was ruthless, greedy and it seemed he'd do anything to get ahead. I thought he wanted to use me to get close to my father. In the end he was sacked for harassment and we had to have a restraining order issued. Anthony said sorry, and explained away his question by saying it was a name he'd heard around the office.

To show his commitment to Finopia, Anthony had decided to make his last deal buying shares in the bank itself. He was going to use most of what he'd earned, the salary he'd saved and his bonuses. He knew he couldn't lose and he thought it would impress Celeste and her father. And, sure enough, after his trade, shares in the bank suddenly rose in value by a fifth. He had hit the target again, made a lot of money and so had everyone else with a stake in Finopia.

But, before he could enjoy it, he had to survive the last trade. He knew it was outside his control and waited nervously to hear from the dark web, which seemed ever more like the dark forest of folklore.

When word came it wasn't what he expected.

There was no final deal, that was just a device, a misdirection to draw him in and focus his mind. The contact had taken payment all along, with a cut from each deal. More than that, explained the contact, his pleasure came from speculating on people, as much as corporations, to see who would perform. Anthony had. But now all traces of contact had to be removed. Anthony was told to delete the programme lose-cipher.exe. Clicking 'uninstall' the screen of his laptop went black and all the small coloured lights showing its functions dimmed and died. Well, smiled Anthony, slightly surprised, a dead portable computer is a small price to pay for all I've gained.

He thought little more about it and went out for a drink to celebrate. There at the bar was Casper. Still smirking but no longer looking agitated. In fact, he looked more pleased with himself than usual, if that was possible. Oddly he seemed to be expecting him, but Anthony didn't expect what was about to wash over his life, and the lives of everyone he knew and many, many others besides.

Casper had reason to be relieved. By clicking 'uninstall', Anthony had inadvertently released him from his darkest deal. The contact on the dark web was known as 'the great speculator', who some thought an urban myth. But he was real and preyed on the naïve and ambitious, as Casper once had been. He'd make a deal with you for instant, fabulous success, but in return, unless you could deliver to him another reckless eager soul by the end of your trades, he would destroy you, everything, and every friend or family member you were connected to.

The trick was, that even to know this much, you would have had to actually read the 75 pages of terms, before ticking to say you had read, understood and accepted them when installing 'lose-cipher.exe.' But who, ever, actually reads those things before accepting them? Casper, a fairly sharp operator, had copied and kept terms, but checked them only later. As Casper confessed all this, with trademark smirk, Anthony's phone began to vibrate with calls, messages and news alerts. He realised Casper must have chosen him as his mark once he had mentioned Celeste's name. Frightened for himself and frustrated by her, picking on Anthony must have seemed perfect.

For the next few hours, Anthony's phone was like a bell tolling the end of days. Through Anthony's synchronised phone and email contacts, the Great Speculator's viral programme emptied the bank accounts of everyone he knew, leaving a message saying that Anthony thanked them for their kind gift.

'What's going on?' pleaded a hundred messages or

more, including, even, one from his mother. Then there was the red banner of breaking news like lava flow from a volcanic economic eruption, spreading across websites and television channels.

He was no longer living a dream, but a nightmare, and he wasn't flying but falling. His magic, speculative, financial bullets were hitting everything and everyone in his life, but were very wide of the target of his success and happiness.

Solar Age had suddenly and unexpectedly gone into receivership when rumours spread that it was over-leveraged and loans were called in. DRIP in India ran dry, bankrupted after a major contamination incident killed thousands in Mumbai, the result of health and safety corner-cutting following pressure to meet investors' expectations. The residents of 380 Care4U homes were made homeless overnight when it emerged that the sale had been under-priced, and identified as a massive asset-stripping opportunity. The buyers had no intention of providing unprofitable long-term care, but saw surplus land for development, possible under new looser planning rules, for sale to international property speculators and money launderers. The official response, rather than accept any responsibility, was to say it was the duty of friends, neighbours and family to take in the homeless, distressed and infirm until other arrangements could be made.

So much was happening, so quickly, that news programmes were extended with special features on 'market madness night'. Maladministration and the cost of private finance initiatives saw the closure of a whole series of academy schools and health facilities, which neither government ministers nor investors were available to be interviewed for on the rolling news.

Anthony was reeling, but a message from Celeste broke through his daze. She had to speak to him. Dealing in Finopia's shares had been suspended. Massive trading losses had been discovered hidden by an anonymous trader in a secret error account numbered 66666.

Celeste was devastated. She had planned to tell him that Finopia was about to make history for a much better reason. She had persuaded her father to create a legacy and set an example to the financial world by converting Finopia into the City's largest, exclusively ethical and environmental investment house. Now that was ruined and the news was triggering a wider crash. What was going on, asked the bewildered journalists? Anthony knew, but he couldn't say.

Instead of creating and making things, like in his

boyhood dreams, trusting to the magic of the market and self-seeking finance, he had broken and destroyed them. Rather than firing magic bullets he felt like he had released a cloud of poison gas.

Celeste insisted they meet. Anthony prepared a speech, part admission, but mostly the final plea of a condemned man, one that even he wasn't sure he would grant if he was pleading with himself. But he couldn't have expected what actually happened. Celeste looked at him with sympathy, saying that she understood, and knew everything.

Anthony was thrown, and found that hard to believe. Celeste explained that after he'd mentioned Casper's name, she'd been frightened because of what happened before, and suspicious so had a private investigator track him to see what he was doing, and whether he was breaking the terms of the restraining order. The investigator had been at the bar when Casper made his admission and taped the conversation.

Celeste could see that Anthony had been manipulated in a complex revenge plot by a bitter and jealous Casper, who had sought to defraud and ruin them both. Anthony was perhaps naïve and misled but, she thought, ultimately blameless. She had passed evidence of Casper's deception, insider trading and distribution of malware to the Serious

Fraud Office who should, at that moment, be arresting him. Casper's later ranting in court about the dark web and the role of the 'great speculator' would later be dismissed with derision by the judge who sentenced him to a lengthy prison sentence.

It was, said the judge, a 'pathetic and transparent attempt, typical of the greedy, status obsessed and adrenalin-fuelled world of finance to deny responsibility for the consequences of its actions.' In a phrase that echoed through media coverage of the case, the judged passed sentence saying that he was a man 'who had sold his soul just to gaze through a hole in a wall for years to come.' It was time to make an example and 'signal a new determination to properly punish the white collar crimes of the rich.'

The tapes also made Celeste realise how much Anthony loved her, so they stayed together through the turmoil. In fact, using Celeste's skill at raising finance and environmental interest, Anthony even found himself helping to create something out of nothing. Together, they created an enormously successful crowd-funder for community owned renewable energy co-operatives.

As if by magic, resistance to such schemes melted away because local people were making the decisions and taking the benefits. Wind and solar power appeared across the country like the conjured meadows and trees of Anthony's childhood dreams.

And, at that moment, not far away in Whitehall, deep in the Treasury, a newly installed, young and ambitious Chancellor of the Exchequer, sat at his computer, slightly drunk with surprise at his own success, but feeling he deserved it, and wondering what he could do to beat it.

He had left the world of finance at the right moment to avoid blame, and risen as others fell during the market chaos. Idly, he noticed a very black pigeon land outside his window. Once upon a time these birds lived wild on cliff faces. Big city buildings to them were an opportunity.

He had got where he was by taking political risks and spotting opportunities, and decided to take another when he turned back to his personal laptop computer and clicked to install a new programme – lose-cipher.exe.

12

The Drowning of Doggerland

Jules Pretty

It begins: an ancient fray, falling rain, the birds had flown. The land had been dry, but now came flood. Pull up a stool, this tale is of The People and takes some telling. Fetch another log, fire up those flames, come closer, leave those shadows.

It had been fearsome cold, tundra-chilled far south.

Time passed, paused, The People padded north, mammoth fewer now,

Hunting hill and grassy plain of Doggerland,

They camped at salty-marsh and lashed lagoon, by a million whistling waders.

At some centre lay Asgard, land of gods, ash Yggdrasil propping up the sky.

At edge, Utgard, beyond ditch and wave-defence, the serpent-circled sea

Where giants gathered, troll teeth glistening in the dark.

In those days, Dogger was a wide dry land.

These mesoliths stalked the horse and stamping auroch,
Red deer, bison, haired rhinoceros, reindeer harried by their dogs.
They fished the shore for shell, fixed barb of antler bone,
Laid long lines, hauled in fish; there was no wheat nor tamed cow.
For a thousand years, ten hundred more, they hunted tunnel valley,
Roamed plain, fished flats, sharpened spearpoint, sang their sagas.
The gather-hunters had shaped their land, sowing seed and fruit,
Harboured plants by house and clearing,
They did not wish for any better place.

Now came a steady shift, a warmer era, glacier melting, floe and iceberg breaking free, the seas filling up. Did they sense a fear, would the weft of salty sea shift their ways? Their fire-dragons dozed in deeps, boilers blue, silent now for centuries. Their eagles lazed, cloud-high, serene along the stormy shore. All waves were friends, but soon would not. A great betrayal was soon to come.

Sky-Ryder was a wiry wanderer, their leader.

    The People's herald, she sang their life-story.

    Sun-scorched skin, two clasping amber brooches,

    Loose-limbed still, she led the tribe

    Across ripped steppe and marsh, watched light pass away to northern sea.

    They chattered by the flickered fire, at the yurtish camp,

    Tossed laughing infants in the air, never weary.

    Days would always pass, years too, grey hair did always come.

Yet as the gannet cried, curlew wheeped, a storm was beating at the cliff.

    Grand-daughter Sky-Shire, shaman-dreamer too,

    Saw water at the swamp, serpent could no longer hold the tide.

    And from the hot-lands hurried whispers, those herding people paused,

    Had broadcast emmer-einkorn, raised walls, tamed their cattles.

    Still the Dogger People sang of hunts, hero-honed the sharper blade,

    Battled bear and browser; it had always been this way.

Now waves were rolling, rising, breaking, the height
of her in half a hundred years.

Inward and upslope they carried camps, buried
bones again.

Where their great-grandmothers had nursed the
flame, crooned lullaby,

So advanced the lapping wave, the curling
current,

They had always moved, just now shifted sooner:
the Skys were not alarmed.

Yet soon salt-flushed the wooded vale of Silver
Pit;

Can you imagine, herring soon would follow.

How terrible, when the wealth of worlds is laid to
waste, when tent-skins have become rime-encrusted,
when waves bind all our bones. This is a reminder:
our own chill winters fast approach.

Gulls seethed around the shore, petrel plunged.

Cold cormorant of Utrost cried, Sky-Shire knew it
was another sign.

They could not tame the tempest, even serpent
tired.

Their long dry land had shrunk, a narrow breach
at first,

Then widening yeasty sea, grave, plain, lane all lost.

They could wade across, hurried hide-boat and birch-canoe.

But now a shocking sight: the sun rose from water, set too in waves.

When the night-lion roars, your senses sharpen.

For this was growling sea: tide took land, did not retire.

Plain became marsh then subsided, poplar, birch, ash now salt-kilt.

All searched above for signs, the stars and moon and sun,

Watched cloud and soul-bird, tallied days long and short,

Watched burning streak cross moonlit sky.

Sky-Shire sent scout with walking dog, they knew the celestial skies.

They returned with news: they were surrounded.

They would have to learn a wet world now.

Sky-Shire was taller than her mother, taller too than Sky-Ryder,

She stood before their yurts and spirits,

Said, we must dig up a hundred holy graves,

Carry ancestor bone, ash-bow, bear tooth,

Bury again, seal flipper, red-deer skull, axe and

antler harpoon

She called aloud: stop, desist. Still storm surged,

Poured inland for league on league; never letting up.

Midden limpet and periwinkle, whelk and oyster returned to salty sea,

Now they chewed on wrasse and saithe, long ling too.

She shrank with age, now Dogger Isle was disappearing.

From Ceres slope and desert plain, trade joined the transformation.

Grassy seed, it made them gasp: now landscapes shrunk again.

Select your docile beast, said traders, you need them by your tent.

And brought smaller cow, woodland-pig, woolly sheep for every hill.

The proud People, wild-horse hunter, elk-stalker, beaver-trapper,

Shuffled behind Sky-shaman, skulls with antlers wide, tied to heads.

They carried bruised blade of flint, axe and adze, spear and arrow point.

They still were made for walking;

Ranging now from wet to higher land, behind them washed another wave.

They abandoned gods: they could see they failed this test.

It was their trail of only tears.

One grey day of mist, the west wall of vast Valhalla fell, shear slid, Storegga tumbled, three mountains rock on rock in water. A tsunami raced south and west, burst Lake Agassiz. It poured across the final flats, washed upslope, over mound, around the back. Now the middle land was shallow sea. Doggerland was fishground, sand bank, swale and swatchway, watery pit. Cod and herring shoaled where deer and horse had shone.

I see the fire splutters now, your children are asleep. Now heed this story, set a sentry, that sea did stop. But Sky-Shire and her Dogger People did not know it would. They worshipped land and plant, fish and fowl, yet their land became a watery grave, a novel northern sea. Do you have a hacker-code, do you have the ear of gods today? Look. Can you hear wind roar, have you been outwitted?

Look, maybe not. For now, let us sing of sagas of the north, how we faced a sea that once was land.

13

The flower that made monkeys screech at night

Chris Nichols

The old woman settled herself for her work on the high moon-flooded rock, her sleeping village far below.

She began to beat a gentle rapid rhythm on her drum. She enjoyed looking out over the night valley, her closed eyes seeing far. She had work to do. There were questions to be answered ...

Long before you reach the cool of the tea-plantation hills, you might take the rarely trodden track deeper into the forest.

If you do, thick vegetation closes behind you like a curtain at every turn. The breath of the jungle weighs down, a damp presence clinging to your back.

Maybe the sense of the forest closing in would deter you. Maybe the heat would wear you down. Maybe the strange cries from the forest canopy would cause you to turn and flee. Some would go on.

If you did, for many hours and many miles, you would come to the valley of the Junjatika.

The Junjatika had lived in the valley for generations too many to count. Here they belonged. Here they raised young, hunted and gathered, told stories and sang and made pots of rich clay. The valley appeared unchanging. This was the valley of their stories. They were woven into the valley and their lives were woven by it.

Then, in the seventieth summer of the life of Nanaja, an elder woman of the village, something changed.

In the month without rain, when the moon was full, a strange flower began to appear in the valley. It was a large flower with petals that clung tall together, upright in the heat of noon, and at night spread wide like a star. When open, the inner side of the flower was luscious purple, a densely seeded heart. The sticky sap filled the valley with a honeyed scent almost unbearable to the senses.

The flowers bloomed for thirty-three nights, and then were gone until the next year, appearing once again when the full moon shone in the month without rain.

The first time the flowers appeared the villagers were curious. There were one or two flowers, nothing more. By the third year of the flowers coming, they filled the valley floor during the days and nights of their strange blooming.

By the next year, the villages came to Nanaja saying:

'We must kill the flowers, cut them down....'

'We must stop them seeding...'

'Let us burn the valley floor and let new green shoots come...'

Nanaja listened and heard their fear.

The flowers did have their effect on the valley. The sweet stench drove away the animals from the valley and while the flowers bloomed the hunting was poor. The children went hungry during the days of the blooming. Worst of all, the perfume of deep sticky sweetness drove wildness into the hearts of the canopy monkeys, who would screech and yell through the nights of the flowering. No one could sleep while the flowers filled the valley.

So Nanaja went to the high rock. She looked over the valley, eyes closed, and drummed, as she had done decade upon decade, drumming for wisdom to come to her as it always did.

Her spirit was stirred by the drumming and, as was her gift, she left her body and soared. Soon she was skimming over the canopy of the forest, her skin cool in the night air of the tree tops. Then she swept down, deep to the forest floor, into the steam of night.

Here the seedlings of the purple night star were beginning their journey to the light, the flower buds already forming. In a few days, their flowering would come about. Nanaja spoke with the spirits of the plants, and with their help, she saw.

She saw the joy of the brief flowering, the pregnancy of the bud, the joy in the immense purple spreading. She felt life flowing in the thick sticky seed head and almost recoiled in her flight at the closeness of its scent.

In her eyeless flight, she saw the bugs that came to feed on the sap and seeds. She saw dark, shelled creatures of the deep earth, laborious at the flower heads, feasting, moving on, carrying pollen as they fed on the rich sweetness. Then she saw the rainbow winged birds, the rare and secretive feeders that preyed upon the bugs and spread the seeds of the flower in this valley and beyond.

As she watched, she understood her oneness with the rainbow winged birds, with their delicate probing beaks; her oneness with the scrabbling bugs, and her oneness with the strange and wonderful flower and with its brief blooming gift of new seeds, new foods and new life. Nanaja's spirit soared ever more at one with the forest, the canopy, the night creatures and the stars overhead, all lit by sister moon in her wonder.

She returned to her body knowing that her questions had been answered.

The people of the village came again to Nanaja.

'We must act now,' they said to her. 'We have to burn the flowers or we will have no peace at night, we will have no food …. Our children will go hungry again.' …

She sat in the firelight waiting for the circle to fall quiet. When it did, she spoke.

'I have travelled with the spirits,' she said. 'The purple night star flowers are our brothers and sisters. We will share the valley with them.'

She could see that the villagers were still troubled. She went on.

'Long, long ago, this valley was not our home. Our ancestors' ancestors arrived here long before the dawn of our stories. We were like the purple night star. When we walked, the forest felt our strangeness and heard us breaking its silence. The trees and animals did not drive us out. They fed us and took us to their heart.'

Nanaja saw that some of the older heads nodded.

'What about our hunting?' said the warriors? 'The stench chases out the animals.'

'We cannot gather seeds and berries,' said the gatherers. 'We cannot walk the paths we know because of the carpet of strange flowers.'

'What about our sleep?' said the oldest man. 'The monkey cries deny me rest and I fear the wakeful hours of the night.'

After a silence, Nanaja spoke again.

'Let the time of the full moon in the month of no rain be a time of celebration for us. Let us not hunt in these days, nor gather berries from our usual paths. Let us fast, or else eat new berries gathered from different places.'

She rested, watching the flicker of the fire.

'The bloom of the night star is brief,' she said. 'Its short time of flower reminds us of our own brief flowering. None of us has many moons to live in this valley. None of us have moons enough to drive out the life of others. The forest is not ours. We share it with the flower, with the shelly bug and the rainbow winged bird. Let us make the brief blooming a time to celebrate a new flowering.'

Nanaja noticed the deep silence around the fire and she knew that the people heard her story.

'We are a fragile people,' she said 'and we fear our

own fragility. We fear that the coming of the strange flower will break the known ways. But life itself is stronger than our thin skin. Life is hungry and always finding new ways. Let us hold out our arms in welcome and see the wonders in our midst.'

She turned to the oldest man and spoke.

'I too am old and share your love of sleep... But we both will soon sleep long enough to cure all ills. The crazy calling of the monkey lasts only while the flower blooms. Let us, you and I, not sleep on those nights but join the canopy monkeys in their screeching. Let us make these nights a time of music and life for us just as the monkeys dance and sing in the high places of the forest. Let us, even the oldest and closest to death, share in the joy of the new and the most alive.'

Nanaja looked into the eyes of the old man and saw his tears.

'You are right,' he said softly to her. 'I fear the dark night that is pressing ever more on me.'

The villagers looked at the two elders sitting silently in the firelight and were themselves decided. The purple night star was part of the new life of the valley just as the Junjatika themselves had once seeded as new life on this soil. Now they too saw that their lives, their stories, their pots thrown from the rich clay – all of these were themselves a new blooming in their turn. Without the strangeness of renewal, all of their lives and stories each would fail and fade to dust.

At the full moon in the month of no rain, Nanja took herself to the high rock above the village. The air was filled with the dense sweet stench of the purple night star, as the plants stretched out their flowers into the forest night. Below, she knew that many of the villagers were fasting, whilst others feasted on strange berries gathered on new paths.

Nanaja's closed eyes saw the light of the celebration fire burning in the hearts of the villagers. She could see the dancers moving in the firelight and hear their yells and calls as they joined the canopy-monkeys in their frenzy.

She picked up her drum and began her steady beat. As was her gift, she became the oneness. She licked the sweet sap from the centre of the flower and tasted its power, and she danced screeching in the canopy of the forest.

14

The Baba Yaga's mission

Sarah Deco

The Baba Yaga pushed open the shining glass doors of the shopping centre. She stood inside, between the marble wall of the department store and the long glass windows of the supermarket, and listened. Yes, the atmosphere was alive with the sounds of distressed children. Crying whining children, angry screaming children, bored toddlers. The air was thick with their misery. Good! It would be easy pickings.

The Baba Yaga rummaged in her shopping bag on wheels and sang a song to herself in a voice as creaky as an old barn door.

'Fie, fie, fiddly, diddly, dum, I smell the soul of a sad little one.'

She sat herself down on a red leatherette sofa, and spread her coat out. Her old brown coat had far too many pockets, out of which you might see if you looked closely, little things peep out. Creeping crawling things; beetles, worms, centipedes and worse. She took a wide-mouthed flask out of her shopping bag, unscrewed it and holding it in both knobbly hands, waited.

A woman with a cross face and tight trousers, pushed a buggy towards where the Baba Yaga sat. The small child in the buggy was screaming. Trussed like a roasting bird his arms pinned by the buggy straps, he wriggled and wailed.

The Baba Yaga yawned. She didn't even need to make an effort these days. Children were so unhappy and their parents so stressed, the job was almost done for her.

'Shut up!' said the tight faced mother as she hurried the buggy along the crowded mall past the Baba Yaga.

As they came close, the Yaga uncurled her knobbly finger, focused her beady eyes and whispered,

'Come to me... I will tell you a story...'

A small sphere of light, like a shining blue green bubble drifted up out of the child's chest. It floated in the air, turning like a planet in slow orbit and came to rest in the palm of The Yaga's hand. The Baba Yaga plopped it into the flask and screwed the lid on, as the mother pushed the buggy onwards and out of the shopping centre.

Once upon a time when children ran in the wild

forest, their souls were almost impossible to capture. Hard as diamonds they were and just as bright. Children then knew all the stories, how to outwit a troll, confuse a Nix. They knew never to go home with a fairy or a Baba Yaga, but now... well...

'Ah here's another one,' she thought, rummaging in her shopping bag for a sweet, just in case she needed any extra persuasion. But no, this one was... Oh, this two! A twin buggy! A very fancy contraption, double buggy with iPad holders.

The little ones were sitting with glazed eyes in front of screens. Tinny sounding things blaring out synthesised nursery tunes.

The Yaga smiled, her once toothless jaws were now filled with brilliant white teeth, courtesy of cosmetic dentistry. Her nose no longer met her chin, but sat pertly on her taught face. Her warts had been sheared off with a scalpel.

'What a lovely pram,' she said to the perfectly coiffed mother. 'Where *did* you get it from?'

'Oh, It's a super deluxe model from Chic Maman baby boutique.'

'Is it really?' said the Yaga Baba. She waved a sweet between one of the children and the screen that was perched in front of his face. She caught his attention and woof, out came the soul.

Children, as everyone knows, are hungry for

stories. Their ears prick up at the sound of a Yaga's approach. They know this means a proper tale, one with a challenge. One that will make them stronger.

The Baba Yaga scanned the concourse with her small bright eyes.

'That's a sad little one over there' the witch said to herself. 'Perhaps a bit too old, but worth a try.'

She stood up and walked across the shiny marble floor towards a small blonde boy sitting on a bench swinging his legs and looking at the floor. As she walked past him she whispered,

'Once upon a time... in a land far away,'

A blue green bubble emerged briefly from his chest hovered in the air between them, appeared uncertain of where to go, and slipped back silently inside the boy's body. The child lifted his head and looked at her, straight in her eyes.

'What're you doing?' he said accusingly.

'What am *I* doing?' she said innocently. 'I'm doing nothing but shopping as everyone does who comes here.'

'I don't,' he said.

'What are you doing her then, my dear young man?'

'I'm not your young man,' he said, crossing his arms belligerently. 'You're doing something funny with that thing, that thing in your bag and the babies, I saw you'

'I don't know what you mean,' she said beginning to walk towards the door.

The boy slid off the bench and was now walking along beside her.

'I'm gonna see what you've got in there,' he said pointing to her basket on wheels.

'You certainly are not. Where is your mother?'

'Don't have one.'

'Well, who looks after you?'

'My aunt, but she's ill.'

The Baba Yaga was walking as fast as she could but the boy was keeping up. She wished she still had her mortar to ride around in. She could really push that thing with the pestle. It moved like the wind, like a tornado, but, this was no time for nostalgia.

'I'm going home now and you are going to find your aunt.'

'I told you she's ill; she drinks too much.'

'And your father?'

'Busy.'

'He'll stop being busy soon and wonder where you are.'

'He's busy in Russia.'

'In Russia?' The Baba Yaga slowed her pace.

'Moscow.'

'What's your name, child?'

'Vassily.'

'Fie, fie,' she said to herself. 'I thought I smelt the blood of a Russian one.'

'Why are you not in Russia with your father?'

'My mum died. He went back to Russia.'

'Right young man, this is my bus stop. You must go home.'

Vassily didn't move.

'Go home!'

He stayed put. The bus drew up. The doors swung open. The Baba Yaga lifted her shopping trolley on to the bus and sat down.

A few moments later she felt a tap on her shoulder. It was Vassily in the seat behind her grinning. She ignored him.

`When the bus reached her stop on Dudden Hill Lane, she tried to sprint for the exit. Despite her efforts, Vassily was still there beside her as she walked along Colin Road and arrived at her door.

'You can't live here.' he said.

'Why not?'

'It's a warehouse, sort of factory thing.'

'Is it indeed? Goodbye, Vassily,' she said firmly.

Children used to run from her in terror. Her name had only to be mentioned for them to run away screaming.

She unlocked the door and walked into the

cramped hallway that led through to the great dark space she now called home. Vassily slipped inside like a shadow and silently followed her. As they came into the warehouse, he saw a bed by the wall and dived quietly underneath it.

Huge humming tanks rose from the floor to the high ceiling. In them hung little blue green spheres, suspended in amber jelly. They cast a mellow light, like stained glass windows, over the formica kitchenette and the table.

The Baba Yaga put the kettle on, took off her coat, hung it on a metal hook and took the flask out of her shopping bag. Holding it tightly she began to climb the long iron ladder that led all the way to the top of the tanks.

Vassily slipped out from his hiding place, watched her climb for a moment and then walked towards her coat. He began to investigate its pockets. Slimy creatures poked inquisitive noses and antennae out at him. He jumped back as a lizard bit his finger. He poked inside a pocket out of which dropped bits of twig and creeper, a baby crow flew out brushing him with its wings. It cawed loudly in his ear and then flew up into the rafters.

When the Baba Yaga reached the last rung of the ladder, she opened a metal flap on the top of the tank. She unscrewed the flask and tipped the contents in. 'What are they,' said Vassily, shouting up at her.

'Are you still here? I thought I'd got rid of you.'

'Tell me, what they are, those shiny round things?'

'They are souls, Vassily.'

'What are souls?'

'Didn't anyone ever talk to you about your soul?'

'No, don't think so'

The Yaga sighed as she climbed down the ladder.

'I don't know' she said. 'What a world!'

'Have you got any food?' said Vassily.

'You want me to feed you now child, have you got no shame? There's cabbage soup on the stove, heat it up.'

Vassily leapt to it with the air of a child well used to fending for himself.

'Tell me, Russian child. Are you fleeing a deed, or doing a deed?'

'What?' he said, stirring the lumps of potato and cabbage in the big pot.

'Have you never heard,' she said, 'the story of the Witch Baba Yaga, who lives in a house in the forest, that stands on chicken's legs?'

'No, sounds like a stupid story.'

The Baba Yaga sighed. She felt the weight of how big was the task ahead of her.

She had made the journey from Russia with the

help of the trolls. Now they shared the warehouse with her. Behind the metal wall that divided the warehouse space, they would be busy staring into their screens.

'Why are you doing that?' Vassily said. 'Stealing souls?'

'You ask too many questions boy. Children who ask questions get old too soon.'

Vassily shovelled the soup into his mouth with enthusiasm.

The Yaga missed her old iron stove, in which, legend had it, she cooked small boys, and her wooden bed hung with felt curtains. She missed her servants. The three pairs of disembodied hands that would wait in the air to do her bidding. And the three fine riders, white, red and black that heralded the turning of the world.

'I'm rescuing souls, Vassily, because the world is very much changed and, until it's either changed back or changed forward, souls are in peril.'

'But you're a witch!'

'I am *The* witch.'

'Witches are evil,' he said screwing up his eyes at her.

'Ach! Evil schmeevil! Who these days knows which is what?'

Vassily took a bit of bread and dipped it in his

soup. 'You like that soup? she said. 'I see you've finished it.'

Vassily nodded.

The trolls next door were chattering louder now. She could hear their banter and their angry carping voices and rabid key tapping. It made her shudder when she heard the trolls going about their business. Then all at once, a sound like fighting cats, or wolves howling in the night, came roaring through the metal partition.

The Baba Yaga banged on the concertinaed metal wall.

'Zamohlchee! Shut up! Aach what a noise they make!'

The partition opened a crack, squeaking and squealing like an animal in pain. A small goblin stood there in the gap, on guard.

Vassily looked at the goblin with his mouth open. Then he stared past him at the rows of computer screens. Behind each one was a grey wrinkly troll. The blue light of the screens shed a ghastly glow on their red eyes. Vassily could see that the floor under the trolls was covered with empty sweet wrappers, crisp packets, beer cans, the remains of pizzas and other takeaways. Each troll had something in his hand he was eating. One absent mindedly picked up a rat that was skittering across the debris, stuffed it in his mouth and chewed.

Vassily shuddered.

'*Zamohlchee*! Be quiet, wretched creatures,' the Baba Yaga shouted past the goblin.

'Yes mother, sorry about that.' he said. 'The boys were celebrating.' The wall squealed shut.

'What are they doing in there?' said Vassily

'A little bit of hate, a few lies, eye of newt and toe of toad, leg of a cockatrice and a few basilisk's teeth, and there you are, false news, fake truth and poison. Internet trolls creating havoc.'

Vassily chewed his bread. 'My aunt says the world's fucked,' he said.

'Does she indeed and what do you think?'

Vassily shrugged.

'The trolls say,' said Baba Yaga, 'that the internet is where all the best nightmares are these days. Got to keep up with the times, they say. 'A drop of falsehood, a measure of slander and a sprinkle of deadly nightshade and stir it all up.' I have to say, I don't like it. I don't like it at all. Come Vassily let me show you something.'

She walked to her coat, hanging on its hook, and reached inside what looked like a very deep pocket. She pulled out a round mirror, around its frame wound silver snakes and green vines.

'Look into this Vassily and tell me what you see.'

He could see nothing but darkness, but slowly the black turned to deep green, he began to make out the trunks of tall trees, branches and leaves. He could hear birds singing and crows calling. He saw green shoots rise from the forest floor and turn into flowers, mushrooms pushing up through the leaves. He saw mice and rabbits, squirrels and birds.

'It's a wood,' he said. 'A very big wood.'

'It's wild forest,' she said.

Vassily carried on looking, his eyes bright and eager. A grey shaggy creature, emerged out of the shadows, looked at Vassily and walked off. A boar with tusks grunted and sniffed and finally a bear came towards him, stood on its hind legs and roared.

Vassily dropped the mirror. 'What was that?'

'That was a bear.'

'And where is that?'

'My home.'

'Wah, awesome!'

'It is indeed.'

'Can I go there?' said Vassily his eyes shining.

'Who knows, Vassily.'

'Please, will you take me there?'

'Time to go home now, Vassily.'

'Can I come back tomorrow?'

She thought for a moment.

'Perhaps.'

It was quiet now. When the hum of the generator paused, she could hear the souls singing; quiet as the flutter of a sparrows wing, or the murmur of a stream.

She picked up a ball of wool and her needles and began to knit.

One day, when the time was right, when wilderness once more thrived undisturbed, the souls would wake. She could go home then, dust off the skulls on her fence posts and see them shine their ghoulish light.

She rocked and knitted, rocked and knitted the threads together, repairing as best she could the tears in the fabric of the world. The wild can survive without man, but his soul won't survive long without the wild. Grandmothers and Baba Yagas know these things.

15

Of gods and men

Geoff Mead

The world was no longer young when Nanahuatl took to the sky. Four different suns had come and gone before the god of earthquakes rose in the house of dawn and blazed across the heavens. It was in this time that the creator Queztalcoatl stole bones from the Land of the Dead. He gave them to Snake Woman who ground them to powder in a jade bowl. Then Queztalcoatl and the other spirits mixed their own blood with the powder to give life to the people, saying: 'We bled for them and they will bleed for us.'

Queztalcoatl cracked open Food Mountain and gave the people true corn, peppers, beans, sage and all that they needed to live. The first people to have many children were the Toltecs; they worshipped Queztalcoatl and they built a great pyramid for him in their capital Tula, so he could dwell amongst them. In return, he gave them all manner of skills: the reading of omens, the making of calendars and pots, farming, weaving, and warfare. He taught them how to find jade and turquoise and other precious stones inside ordinary rocks.

The Toltecs were rich, their cities great, and food was plentiful. Their vegetables grew as tall as trees, their ears of corn so fat that a man could carry only one at a time. They had chocolate, and cotton plants that grew in every colour of the rainbow. For centuries, inside his pyramid, Queztalcoatl accepted the blood sacrifices of his chosen people as his due. It was how things should be arranged between gods and men. But both men and gods can become complacent.

Queztalcoatl's twin, the destroyer Tezcatlipoca, looked down upon them from the sky and was jealous. 'They have forgotten me,' he said. 'There is no light without shadow. Perhaps it is time for me to remind them who I am.' He gathered spiders' webs and twisted them into rope, tied one end to a cloud and climbed down it until he stood outside the gates of Tula. There he changed himself into a wild man and walked bare-naked into the city, with a bag of chili peppers slung over his shoulder. He squatted in the market place, laid out the peppers on the ground and offered them for sale to the small crowd that gathered around him.

It so happened that the king's daughter, Jade

Skirt, was walking through the marketplace with her serving women. She was beautiful and much admired by all Toltec men, but her father King Huemac kept her close by his side and despite many rich offers, would give her to no-one. She saw the bare-naked wild man and was immediately overcome with desire for his *tototl*. She returned to the palace hot, flustered and sick with passion.

When her father saw that his daughter was sick, he asked her serving women what was wrong with her. 'It was the wild man selling peppers in the market,' they said. 'He has bewitched her and she is burning for him.'

'Indeed,' said Huemac. 'We'll see about that.' He told his servants to search the marketplace and when they returned empty-handed, he issued a general decree to all Toltecs to look for the wild man. At last he was found and brought before the king.

'Who are you, who has so upset my daughter?'

'I'm just a poor savage, selling a few chili peppers.'

'Put on a loincloth or something. Don't you realise where you are?'

'I always go naked, your majesty. I've never known any different.'

'Naked or not, you've upset my daughter so you must cure her.'

'It wouldn't be right, your majesty. I'm only a pepper man. Better to kill me instead.'

'There's nothing more to be said,' pronounced the king. 'You caused her sickness and you must cure her.' He clapped his hands and servants took the wild man aside, cut his hair, bathed and oiled his skin and tied a loincloth about his waist. When he was presentable, Huemac summoned his daughter. 'She's yours,' he said. So they were married; Tezcatlipoca became the king's son-in-law and Jade Skirt was soon cured.

Before long though, Huemac heard that people were sniggering and mocking him for marrying his precious daughter to a wild man. His courtiers pressed him to do something before his subjects lost all respect for the throne. 'What do you suggest that I do?' he asked.

'Declare war on our enemies at Grass Mountain and send the wild man into the thick of the fighting with the reserves. They're just boys and old men. We'll win the war but he's sure to be killed.'

'And if he isn't killed?'

'Then he'll be a hero. You've nothing to lose.'

So the army marched to Grass Mountain but Huemac's enemies were strong and his army retreated; all but the reserve. Using Tezcatlipoca's voice of power, the wild man rallied the boys and old men under his command: 'Come uncles, brothers, sons. Come.' They swung their war clubs, yelled and charged. Their foes, hearing the blood-curdling cries and seeing such determination, dropped their weapons and ran.

When word of the rout got back to Tula, Huemac ordered his own turquoise-covered shield and head-dress plumed with quetzal feathers to be brought from the armoury as gifts. He went in person to the edge of the city to meet his son-in-law; drums were beaten and conch-shells blown in triumph as Huemac himself painted the victors' faces yellow to honour the occasion. 'You are a most worthy husband to my daughter and a welcome guest under my roof,' he said. The wild man smiled innocently whilst Tezcatlipoca inside him, fought to contain his malice. 'We should celebrate,' he said.

That very night, the king himself announced that there would be dancing. Tezcatlipoca led the way out of the city followed by hundreds of carousing men and women. He beat a pounding rhythm on his drum as the crowd danced wildly, unable to keep their feet still. Further and further from the city he led them; closer and closer to the edge of a canyon. As they bumped and jostled, pranced and leapt, those nearest the edge were pushed over the precipice onto the rocks below. As they died they themselves were turned into rocks upon which more and more people fell and were killed. They seemed not to realise what was happening; it was as though the dancing had made them drunk. Tezcatlipoca screamed with delight: 'Forget me, would you?'

Night after night, they returned to the same spot to dance as if nothing had happened. Tezcatlipoca had the whole of Tula under his spell. The flower of the city's youth fell to their deaths.

When his bloodlust was assuaged, he turned his attention to his age-old rival. Disguising himself as a wizened, white-haired old man, he paid Queztalcoatl a visit in his pyramid. 'What is it grandfather?' asked Queztalcoatl. 'What do you want from me?'

'I want nothing,' said the old man, holding out a bowl of agave wine. 'In fact, I've brought you something.'

'What is it?'

'Medicine. How are you? Tell me, how are you feeling?'

'I've been here so long,' said Queztalcoatl, 'that I can hardly move. I hurt all over.'

'Then, drink this medicine. It will make you better. It will soothe your head and your body. Then it will go to work on your heart and make you think about going away somewhere else.'

'Where?'

'Where the sun rises; where all your aches and pains will go away; where you will feel as young as a child again. Drink the medicine.'

Queztalcoatl made no move to drink.

'Try a little. Just a little,' said the old man, putting the bowl down in front of him.

Queztalcoatl took a sip and then another. 'It tastes good,' he said. 'Makes me feel good, too.' He drank more deeply, draught after draught until he had emptied the bowl. The drunker he got, the more he wept for his years of suffering and the more he yearned to feel young again. As Tezcatlipoca had hoped, he decided to leave Tula and travel to where the sun rises.

Stretching out his arms, Queztalcoatl broke down the walls of his temple and stepped out. He looked around at the half-deserted city that had once been his favourite. There was no sacrifice on the round stone at the foot of the pyramid; of priests and acolytes, there was no sign. His compact with the Toltecs was over. He set fire to the houses and palaces and cast the city's treasure into ravines and canyons; he set free the captive birds and followed them eastward.

Queztalcoatl went on his lonely way. He stood beneath the Old Age Tree; he traversed Stone Crossing; he cast his necklace into the water at Jewel

Spring; at Sleeping Place, his snores were like thunder. He passed between White Woman Mountain and Popocatepetl, and made his way to the sea. When he reached the shore, he wove live snakes together to make a boat and set off across the water towards the house of the dawn.

Still in the guise of an old man, Tezcatlipoca watched Queztalcoatl disappear. Tezcatlipoca smiled a terrible smile, then twisting and turning like a black whirlwind, he shed his mortal form, took on the aspect of an enormous jaguar, licked his lips, and sprang into the sky. With his interfering twin out of the way, mankind would soon worship once again at the altar of destruction.

The mythically fabulous Toltec empire dominated Mesoamerica from about 900 C.E. for approximately 250 years. The Aztecs, who flourished from about 1300 C.E. until they were conquered by the Spanish in 1521 C.E. told this story to explain how a civilisation even greater than their own had declined and collapsed.

Ironically, Montezuma, the last Aztec emperor, convinced that Hernán Cortés was the god Queztalcoatl returning to the world of men, refused to defend his realm, sending gifts instead to welcome the invader's arrival. My version of this story draws heavily on source material provided by mythologist John Bierhorst in The Hungry Woman: Myths and Legends of the Aztecs *(William Morrow & Company, 1984).*

16

The Spell

James Marriott

There's an image in a book that has bewitched me for three decades. The title reads *'Shot from the cannon'* from *Memories of the Mutiny' by F.C. Maude.* The lithograph shows in the foreground a large cannon. A man is strapped across the mouth of the gun. His hands are tied to the wheels of the gun carriage. He is dark skinned and wears a turban. His head is thrown back in the expectation of unbearable pain.

Another figure, with outstretched arm, touches the rear of the canon with a *botefeux* igniting the fuse. The smoke from the gunpowder rises in the still air. To the left of the gunner is an officer, standing ramrod straight in leather boots, sabre at his side, breast sash and peaked cap. It is clear that he is giving the command. In the background there is a huddle of nineteen men, dark skinned, who are prisoners awaiting their deaths. Seconds later, the canon will roar and the man will scream.

The picture is an eyewitness account of the reprisals meted out by the troops of the East India Company on those that had risen against British rule in the First War of Indian Independence. This conflict, that in 1857 ignited across a sub-continent and raged for two years, was called in English 'the Indian Mutiny'. Under the reasoning that these soldiers were 'mutineers', rather than those who had the courage to become freedom fighters, thousands were slaughtered by having a cannon ball blown through their stomachs.

This method of execution was learnt by the British rulers from the Mughal Empire. As the body of the victim was ripped to shreds, and proper burial rendered impossible, the soul had no chance of rest in the afterlife.

Since I first saw the print, it is the image of the officer that has particularly haunted me. What passes through the mind of a man as he gives that order? How can his heart be so steeled that he can calmly undertake an act of such brutality? And what does it do to the thinking and feeling of a man to undergo such a process?

For these violent methods to become common knowledge through prints and press reports, for them to become an acceptable response to rebellion, surely this leaves a mark on British culture? The

British ruling class in India experienced the uprising against them as months of terror. And they perpetrated terror on the 'natives'. Some criticised the means of reprisals, but mostly they were praised. Charles Dickens wrote: 'I wish I were commander-in-chief in India ... I should proclaim to them that I considered my holding that appointment by the leave of God, to mean that I should do my utmost to exterminate the race.'

It seems that these events changed the practice of conducting the rule of empire. Altered what might be called the acceptable level of violence. And the terror cast its spell over all those that lived through it, all their children and all those that come after.

I am standing beside you and we are talking to a small audience at Cotesbach Hall, which has been the house of my father's family since the mid Eighteenth Century. You have explained the history of the East India Company and how this private corporation collapsed into a maelstrom of violence in the rebellions of 1857. I'm explaining the role of William Fredrick Marriott.

At the age of fifteen, he left Rugby School and joined the East India Company army, undergoing training at the Addiscombe Military Seminary in Surrey. In 1838, he was posted to Mumbai – or Bombay as it was known by the British. The following year he was among the troops who invaded Afghanistan on behalf of the company. He was wounded at the Battle of Ghazni.

By the time of the uprisings in 1857, he was married to Fanny Bartholomew and was living in Bombay with four young sons. The details are not clear to me, but it is likely that as an officer he would have fought the Indian rebels and took part in the reprisals that followed, during which the citizens of Delhi were massacred and whole villages razed with men, women and children killed. Perhaps he was in Bombay during those long months? Perhaps he was witness to events such as those reported in the English local press, which read: '*a native officer of the Marine Battalion and a private of the 10th N.I. were blown from guns on the Esplanade.*' Perhaps he too stood by the cannon and gave the orders?

How did the terror alter his mind and imagination? How did it affect his wife and children? Did they too come to see shooting from the cannon as an acceptable level of violence?

As I talk, I can hear my voice quavering, feel my stomach uneasy. I look to you for reassurance. There are several members of my family in the audience. What will their response be to my criticism of our forebear? How tight is the taboo against speaking ill of any long dead relative, especially one with a title like Lieutenant-General? I explain that it intrigues me how the men in our family can have shifted from being vicars to soldiers, from being servants of God to being servants of empire. How does it alter the self image of a man to hold in his hand a gun, not designed to hunt animals, but to kill men and, *in extremis,* women and children? There were five generations of men in our family who were vicars. Overlapping with them, and extending beyond them, were five generations of soldiers. When I was a child, my uncle was an officer in another brutal war of empire, fighting the Mau Mau uprising in Kenya.

Ours is the first generation in which no one has served in the military, in which no body has taken up the gun. Perhaps at some level part of the spell has been broken? Perhaps the level of violence that is acceptable, and direct personal participation in maintaining that level, is changing? Perhaps the relief I feel at the end of our talk comes because we have played some part in the breaking the other half of the spell? Perhaps it has now become more acceptable to talk of these events, to openly criticise the acts of our relatives, to reveal and keep open the wound?

17

Tales I tell my grandchildren

Marion Molteno

How old am I? Seventy-three. Maybe that seems old to you but, actually, I'm far older in the stories I can tell. I go back more than a hundred years to the stories my mother told me about when she was a child, and I intend to be here at least until you're grown up, so the stories go forward too, imagining the world you're going to be living in then. I'm kind of poised on the middle of a see-saw of stories.

A hundred and one years ago my mother was eleven. She was born in Scotland. She lived with her dad but she couldn't remember her mother or her sister, because they both died when she was very young, of TB – tuberculosis, a disease of the lungs. It used to be very common, and one of the lucky things about living now rather than then is that there's a vaccine for TB, so not nearly so many people get it, and even if you do there are antibiotics to treat it, which there weren't a hundred years ago. Her dad was anxious that she too might get TB if they stayed in the cold damp flat they were living in, so he took her off to somewhere with a warm climate where he hoped he could get a better job so that they wouldn't be poor. That's called emigrating – going to another country to try to make a better life for your family – and, in the country you arrive in, you're called an *immigrant.*

So after that, she lived in South Africa, and that's where I was born. By the time I grew up, things were pretty bad there. The government divided people into different categories, depending on where their ancestors had come from – 'white' (originally from Europe), 'black' (African), 'coloured' (mixed background) and 'Indian' – and all the laws favoured the whites, who had most of the land, and much better schools, houses, and so on.

People had to live in separate areas so you couldn't easily meet people from other groups, and it was actually illegal for whites to marry black or coloured people. You can hardly believe such craziness could happen, but it did, and if anyone criticised the government they got in serious trouble, including going to prison. It became dangerous for us to stay, so when we were young grown-ups, just after university, we left our country, just as my mother had left hers, but for a quite different reason

– and we came to Britain.

So you come from a long line of immigrants, and you'll find that a great number of people everywhere do too, if you got back far enough in their stories. It's good to remember that, if you hear people talking as if immigrants are a problem. Actually, they're usually people who didn't just lie down under problems but decided to try and do something about them. A country that gets a lot of immigrants stands a good chance of getting a lot of remarkable people joining their team.

There's a story about my mother that I want to tell you, because although it happened a hundred years ago, it's got a lot to do with the world we live in today. We hear a lot about wars today, and people fleeing from wars, and people hating other people because they're on different sides in a war. Well, when my mother was eleven, a war started in Europe, with Britain and a lot of other countries on one side, and Germany and Austria on the other side.

People called it different names – The Great War, or The War to End All Wars – because it was so terrible they thought none of their governments would ever be so stupid as to start another one. Kathleen – that was my mother's name – and her dad were 6,000 miles away in South Africa, and he could have decided that the war had nothing to do with him. But it was only four years since he had left Scotland, and he felt he should go back and do something to help. So they sailed on a ship all the way from Durban to Plymouth, a journey that took weeks, and it was dangerous because there were German submarines called U-boats that attacked British and American ships. She was scared, but also a bit excited, and she sat at the prow looking out for a periscope so she could become famous by being the first to warn the captain.

They got to Scotland and went to stay at first with her dad's family. All the younger men were away fighting, and a couple of her cousins were nurses looking after wounded soldiers. Her dad was just too old to go and fight, which was lucky because – if he had been sent to where the war was happening – she soon wouldn't have had a dad either.

But there were other kinds of war work that people did. They grew food to feed everyone, and kept the railways running, and worked in factories making ammunition. What her dad did was to set up hostels for men who were working in factories far from their homes. Kathleen went with him. She would go to school for a few months wherever they were, and then they would move on to set up another hostel in the next place. After the school day, she helped him run the hostel, so she was doing war work too. One of her jobs was to take around glasses of Horlick's Malted Milk, and little cakes with pink icing. She got to be a very experienced waitress, but you can get tired of fake pink icing, and after the war was over she would never, ever drink Horlicks Malted Milk.

It was when they were setting up a hostel in the Highlands that they had the biggest adventure of her life so far. It was in a village called Kinlochleven, at the head of a long inlet from the sea, where there was a factory making something hush-hush from the newly invented alloy, aluminium.

About a hundred men worked in the factory, and the hostel was for them. The village was surrounded on three sides by steep mountains, and people said that there was a reservoir up there that provided hydro-electricity for the factory, and a prisoner of war camp, where German prisoners were being put to work building something new, that no one was allowed to talk about. There were always army trucks passing by, heading up into the hills.

By now Kathleen had spent a lot of time hanging around while adults were talking, and everyone seemed to hate the Germans, and told stories of terrible things they had done in Belgium. Just knowing that some of them were up there in the mountains brought the war suddenly closer.

It was winter – the coldest one anyone could remember. The ground froze, temperatures plummeted. Everyone struggled to keep warm. Being surrounded by mountains, the nights closed in early, and the village was very isolated. There wasn't much news of what was happening in the trenches in France, but by now everyone knew it was a disaster. Women knitted socks for the soldiers, but it was hard to imagine that they would do much good.

Then, one dark November night, the worst storm you could ever imagine broke over them. The wind and rain lashed against the walls and roof, as if intent on destroying them. In the middle of all that something truly terrifying happened. Lorries arrived, soldiers came bursting in, and behind them, coming in out of the dark and cold, a crowd of rough, bedraggled men – the prisoner of war camp in the mountains above had been completely flooded out. The prisoners had been bundled into whatever transport could be found, and here they were, billeted on the hostel, huddling in blankets in rows on the floor.

Everyone was up and busy-ing about. Her dad got her going on the Horlicks Malted Milk routine. She was terrified, certain sure she was going to be murdered, but her dad was in charge, and he had a lot of principles that could sometimes be inconvenient. One of them was that you receive people and welcome them, and you never turn away anyone in trouble. These men might be Germans, and prisoners, but they had fled from the storm, and she knew he was going to consider it his duty to treat them as he would have treated anyone else in that position. So she had no choice.

She stepped carefully between the bodies in blankets, trying not to look directly at their faces while handing over the mugs. And then it happened. One of the men raised himself on one elbow and wordlessly beckoned her to come nearer. Mesmerised, terrified, she moved towards him. She was right up next to him before he indicated what he wanted of her. He pulled out from inside his tattered jacket a photograph of a young girl. His daughter, about her own age. He said her name - Karleen.

Kathleen, Karleen.

For years afterwards, she wondered about that girl. Was she also an only child? Did *she* perhaps also only have a dad? And did she ever see him again?

Twenty years later, when Kathleen was grown up and had young children, people began hearing about Hitler and the Nazis in Germany, and what was happening to the Jews. Then she thought again about her German soldier and Karleen, and she wondered – perhaps they were Jews? According to the Nazi government's rules, you only had to have one grandparent who was Jewish to be counted as a Jew, and then most likely you would be sent to a concentration camp. What if Karleen also had young children – did she manage to get any of them out on the Kindertransport, the trains that took Jewish children out to safety in Britain? Did she go alone, losing all their family?

Then there was another war, and once again Britain and Germany were on opposite sides. German bombs fell on British cities, and in the last stages of the war, Britain got back by dropping far more bombs on German cities, reducing them to rubble. And Kathleen thought, if Karleen was not Jewish – if she has lived through the war so far – is she now in one of those cities, terrified, watching the bombs fall?

There have been wars somewhere almost all the years I have been alive, and I've been lucky not to be in one. But through the kind of work I've done I've got to know lots of people who were. For some years I was setting up English classes in London for people who had come from other countries to live there –

immigrants, refugees. Some had fled from wars, others from governments that were persecuting them.

Later, I worked for Save the Children, for short times in different countries, and many places where there had been wars, and there were refugees trying to find somewhere safe. There are so many stories I could tell you about the extraordinary lives of some of the people I got to know.

You've probably heard about Syrian refugees, and people crossing the Mediterranean in small boats, risking their lives? There's one story I wonder if you heard – about a girl who loved swimming. Before the war she used to train regularly, and hoped one day to compete internationally. Then they had to flee. Eventually, she and her family were in one of those boats. It started leaking, and she knew if she did nothing they would all drown. Her sister could also swim, so she and her sister jumped in the water and pushed that boat while they swam, and while those in the boat scooped out the water. They got to the island safely – her strong swimming had saved them.

Later, when she had found a country to settle in, they spotted her talent and she got more training – and made it to the Olympics, as part of an international refugee team.

Imagine if you were someone like her, with an

ordinary life, doing things you were interested in, and one day your mum and dad said: 'It's too dangerous to stay, we have to go.' Imagine you are one of the lucky ones – you get away from those bombs, you get to the coast, you have enough money to pay the people who are selling old boats – so battered that you're really lucky not to drown, and you land on the beach of a small island in Greece, that is swarming with others – *five thousand* people arriving every day.

For a few days till you recover, you're in a refugee camp – there are new ones being set up all the time to handle everyone who is arriving, but you look around you at the miles of tents and you think, if I stay here, I'll be stuck forever. You've risked everything to start a new life – you can't give up now. So you pack a bag – just water and a little food, nothing else – and at night you set off to walk, hoping to get to a country that will take you and let you live like a normal person, get a job, make a home. You come to a border – and you see that they have built a huge fence, and there are policemen with guns patrolling it.

On the other side of that fence, and beyond all the other patrolled borders, there are people saying: We don't want refugees. They'll take away our jobs, and crowd out our schools. Why are they coming anyway? I'll tell you someone who had an answer, and that was an actor in London called Benedict Cumberbatch.

He was in a Shakespeare play, *Hamlet*, and he's so famous that people were paying hundreds of pounds for tickets. Every night when the play was over, and he had finished being Hamlet, he came out in front of the curtain, and said: 'As you go out, we'll be collecting money to help Syrian refugees.' Then he talked about why they were fleeing, and how it could have been us, and how it was everyone's job to help them. And for people who might say 'Why are they coming?' he quoted a poem by a Somali poet:

'*No one puts children in a boat unless the water is safer than the land.*'

Within a short time, those collections after the show raised £150,000, which they gave to Save the Children, to help Syrian refugee children.

Imagine now another German girl, born about ten years after the war when the bombs were dropping and Kathleen wondered if Karleen was there.

Germany was now divided into two countries, East and West, and people couldn't move freely between them. This girl – let's say her name was Angela - was on the East side. When she was seven, a wall was built through the middle of Germany's most important city, Berlin, and no one could cross it. Angela grew up with that wall, and with the police watching constantly to stop people crossing – and she knew that in the end walls don't work. For one day – she was grown up by then – people got so angry that without anyone organising it, they suddenly started smashing that wall down. The two Germanys became one. She gave up her job to go into politics, to help reshape their country.

That's a real story – her name is Angela Merkel, and now she is Germany's Chancellor. Head of the government – the first woman to be that. When the fences were going up against Syrian refugees, she did something very brave, and very important. She said: 'We will not build another wall. Refugees are welcome in Germany.'

It was brave, because she knew it was going to make her unpopular, which is a thing few politicians will risk. A lot of her supporters were very alarmed: 'There are too many refugees,' they said, 'how can Germany accept them all?' And what made it so important that she took that risk is that, by opening the doors, she shifted the discussion from 'How many can we take this time?' and forced people to think about the long term future.

There will continue to be wars and crises that will

make people flee – and it's going to be a continuing challenge to all other countries about how to respond. She didn't come up with a solution, she just said: We know, from Germany's experience, that building walls doesn't work. We have to try to imagine a future where we don't label people as 'us' and 'them', and only the 'us' people are allowed in.

Here's another way to look at what's happening. Think about some of the famous people you have heard of, and you'll be amazed at how many of them were immigrants or refugees. Handel, the greatest English composer, was a German immigrant. Einstein was a refugee, so was Freud. When you were little did you ever read the Mog stories? Then maybe you'll remember that they are by Judith Kerr – she was a refugee from Hitler. Mo Farah, Britain's greatest ever athlete, came to Britain as a child, in a family that was escaping from Somalia's civil war.

We'd be here forever if we started listing the refugees who have been pioneers of science, of music, or have excelled in every sphere of life.

Of course, most refugees are like you and me, just ordinary people. All that's different about them is that they have had to flee from terrible things – and you or I would have fled just as they did, if it was *our* homes the bombs were falling on. All they want is a chance to lead an ordinary life. For some of them, it's a lot worse than that – the awful things that have happened to them have damaged them psychologically, and they need special help. We'd hope someone would help us, if we were in that kind of trouble.

But the reverse also often happens. Sometimes, when people have had to face tough times and take scary decisions to save themselves and their families – and then have had to adjust to life among different people – sometimes all those challenges bring out extraordinary qualities in them, and they contribute more than just ordinarily to their new society.

There may be a lot of people saying negative things about immigrants and refugees, but the opposite is also happening. Everywhere there are people saying what Angela Merkel said – We welcome refugees. We want to imagine a world where we don't put labels on others to divide us. We are all in this together.

It's easy to feel helpless when we hear about big things going wrong in the world. So I want to tell you one last story, that might give you an idea of something you can do.

Years ago, there was an English boy, Jamie, who wanted more than anything to be magician. He learnt loads of magic tricks and started giving shows, but of course he had to get a proper job. After a while he started working in Palestine, campaigning to make life better for people caught up in wars. He learnt to speak Arabic, so he could be useful talking to people and understanding their situation. Then he got to Lebanon, while the Syrian war was going on, and like all the countries nearby, Lebanon had loads more refugees arriving.

There are about one and a half million in Lebanon now, and over four million in the Middle East. No one knows the exact figures – but just compare that with Britain, where the government says it might eventually take in 20,000. Things are so uncertain that people are living wherever they can find a place, like in broken down and overcrowded apartment buildings. Jamie thought about how awful their lives were, and how stressed those children must feel by what they'd gone through, and he decided to cheer things up by giving them magic shows.

Well, you can just imagine – it was the most fun thing that had happened to them since the terrible time they had had to flee. I've seen a photo of some of those children watching his shows, and their faces tell it all – they are spell-bound. Their imaginations are working away, and their brains are trying to figure out how the tricks work, and they forget about the tense things that have been happening.

There was one boy called Aaref, that Jamie says he'll never forget. He's ten, and living in the hills going to a school that some churches have put together for refugees. Somewhat asked him what he liked best about the show, and he just smiled and smiled and said: 'Everything'.

Jamie got so inspired that he gave up his day job so he could do magic shows the whole time.

I love that story, because it's not just that something good happened for the refugee kids – Jamie also got his life's ambition! He's a full time magician now. But there's a snag – see if you can work it out: Who's going to pay him? He's given up his job but he still needs to earn something to live on, and those refugee kids and their parents don't have money for tickets for shows. Sometimes there are organisations that will pay, but if no one can, he's doing them free. But if it's going to last, others need to chip in.

If you and your friends are looking for a way to help refugee kids, see if you can raise some money, and you could fund a couple of shows. Check him out on Google – the project is called *Magic for Smiles,* and he calls himself Jamie Jibberish, because of all the funny words he uses in his show. They're not English words or Arabic, they're the international language of magic. Join him, and make some magic happen.

And if by the time you get to do it, *Magic for Smiles* is sorted, there will be something else, because so many people are coming up with great ideas all the time. You can too.

18

Fletcher and Steve

Katherine Trebeck

Once upon a time, there was a hare. His great skill was to run very fast. Everyone knew him as 'Fletcher the Fast Hare' – his speed was universally famous. And if anyone didn't know about how fast Fletcher could go, Fletcher would tell them – 'I am so fast and that is all that matters – no one is as fast as me, so no one is as important as me.'

Next to Fletcher lived Steve. Steve was a tortoise and he could not go very fast at all. Steve was slow and steady. Steve knew all the trees and rivers and forests and flowers around the kingdom because he was able to see and smell and listen to them as he went around, slow and steady. Steve knew which animals lived where and he was able to visit them for a cup of tea or a beer whenever he wanted, because he had taken the time to make friends with them.

But to Fletcher the Fast Hare, that knowledge and those friendships didn't matter – all Fletcher saw was that Steve was SLOW. Fletcher laughed at him and said: 'Slow animals are not important, slow animals are backward, slow animals should have no say on what goes on in the kingdom.'

Steve wasn't so sure about this. In Steve's slow wanderings around the kingdom, Fletcher would zoom past him. But Steve noticed how Fletcher didn't even see the other animals around him. Fletcher often raced through thickets and came out the other end with scratches on his arms and legs. Sometimes Fletcher would dash past Steve and drop something, such as an empty packet of biscuits or his red hat. Fletcher never stopped – he kept running. So Steve would pick up the litter for him and looked after his hat till Fletcher noticed it was missing. In Fletcher's haste, he sometimes tripped over roots he didn't see and missed a turn off to a beautiful valley. Steve saw how Fletcher the Fast Hare ran so fast that he didn't seem to ever stop and appreciate where he was.

One morning, Fletcher knocked on Steve's door. 'I am so fast' Fletcher said to Steve. 'This quarter, my speed has gone up 1.3 percentage points.' Steve smiled to himself – that same quarter Fletcher had dropped a lot of empty packets of biscuits in his running about. Steve saw the scratches on Fletcher's arms where, in his haste to go faster and faster that quarter, he didn't notice the harm he was doing to himself.

Steve wanted to suggest to Fletcher that he walk with him, that he took the time to visit the beautiful valley Fletcher kept rushing past. That he was careful not to scratch himself and not to drop the empty biscuit packets. But when Steve asked Fletcher to join him for a slow and steady walk around the kingdom, Fletcher laughed: 'I don't care about noticing things along the way. I don't care about the scratches. It doesn't matter if I drop biscuit packets. All that matters is speed.'

So Steve suggested that he and Fletcher have a race. Fletcher thought Steve the Slow and Steady Tortoise must be having a laugh! Fletcher said to Steve: 'I am so fast I bet I can run the race *twice* in the time it takes you to walk it once.' Steve thought: it didn't matter how fast an animal goes, what matters is that they get to where they want to be. So Steve agreed: 'You run the race twice and we'll see who enjoys the finish more.'

Word quickly got around the kingdom that Steve the Slow and Steady Tortoise and Fletcher the Fast Hare were going to have a race.

Animals gathered to watch. Jasper the Journalist Jaguar was ready to report on the times Fletcher and Steve ran – Jasper the Journalist thought this was

163

the most important news story of the year. Ivan the Investor Iguana told people he would build his hotels in the yard of whoever ran the fastest time – Ivan the Investor thought that fast times were the only thing that matter for where buildings should go.

Eventually the day of the race arrived. Steve and Fletcher set off. Steve slow and steady and Fletcher fast and faster and faster.

Fletcher raced around once and began his second lap. Fletcher ran so hard his heart hurt. As he puffed and his legs started to become sore, Fletcher thought: 'How silly Steve is for thinking he can enjoy the finish more than me.'

But Steve was slowly making his way around the course – smiling as he went. He stepped gently over the roots whereas Fletcher tripped over them. Steve paused for a drink at the little river whereas Fletcher rushed past; not even noticing the river existed. Steve visited one of his friends along the way – they gave him some chocolate for energy. Fletcher couldn't ask for chocolate – in his rushing about, he hadn't made friends with any of the other animals.

Steve kept going and soon he could see the destination. He could hear Fletcher on his second lap, coming closer. Fletcher's feet hurt and his arms were scratched – but he didn't mind, he told himself that all that mattered was the speed with which he ran. The animals were cheering – they could see that Fletcher and Steve would reach the destination at the same time. Steve kept walking towards it – a slow, steady pace, waving to his animal friends as he went. Fletcher rushed towards it – eyes down, focused on nothing else than getting there fast.

Fletcher the Fast Hare and Steve the Slow and Steady Tortoise reached the destination almost together, with Fletcher just a few steps in front – the crowds cheered. Jasper started writing the headline for the news. Ivan prepared a prospectus for his investment in Fletcher's yard.

Steve didn't mind that he was slower – he was able to relax with his friends at the destination and properly explore the place he'd been walking towards. He put his feet up and enjoyed a cold beer, breathing the fresh air and listening to the birds in the trees.

But then something terrible happened – Fletcher collapsed. He was so thirsty, his heart was pounding so hard trying to get blood around his arteries fast enough, and his scratches had become so sore, that his body could not take it anymore.

Steve rushed to support him – carrying Fletcher into his house and giving him water and chocolate. Eventually Fletcher regained his strength and could stand up again.

But Fletcher had learnt his lesson – going too fast could be dangerous. From that day on, Fletcher let Steve show him the beautiful valley and introduce him to the animals around the kingdom. Fletcher's scratches healed and he stopped to pick up the empty biscuit packets that he had dropped from all his previous trips racing around the kingdom.

Steve smiled to himself – he and Fletcher were having great adventures together and he knew that Fletcher no longer thought that being fast was all that mattered.

19

There are alternatives

Ed Mayo

A boy is born on Mill Street. Or rather he is driven home to Mill Street from the hospital in town some twelve hours after his birth. The road is a long straight row of terraced houses on both sides built for miners, although mining had long since died in the area.

As the boy grows up, a newsagent, a fish and chip shop, a café and a pet shop are the sources of local entertainment. His father says little but, when he speaks, he is a source of all wisdom to the boy, as fathers often are when their children are young.

When he is not working nights, his father goes to the pub. From time to time on a Friday or a Saturday, the whole family goes down the lane to the Social Club.

One Saturday, the Social Club is having a talk. A councillor, Reg, is talking about the local neighbourhood. Children are chasing sinking balloons on the hall floor, whirling between tables as Reg stands on the stage to speak.

'It's hard. The economy is tricky. It is a time of austerity. The council has to make decisions,' he says, working his way up to the decision that they had come to hear about.

He is talking about spending cuts. A mile away on the road to the big town and the hospital, there is the swimming pool. Always small, always overheated, the pool where the boy was taught to swim is now earmarked for closure.

'There is nothing we can do. That's life,' concludes the councillor, raising his low voice with depressed finality.

The boy who has been listening in once the hall fell silent, as the announcement was made, turns to his father and asks: 'Is that true, dad? Is there no alternative?'

His father puffed on his pipe, turning the ash red, blowing out smoke and drawing breath before replying.

'There is always an alternative, son. There is always an alternative,' his father replies. This fills him with hope.

In his teenage years, big, dyslexic and short-sighted, he is not someone to whom hope comes easily. He struggles to make friends and he struggles in class. His school reports don't predict hope – in fact, they warn of failure. According to the teachers, his attitude is poor, his application is poor, his discipline is poor. He takes exams when the time comes, missing two, failing three and with low results for four. The school calls him in and says it is time to leave.

With no space at home, he leaves. He finds a ground floor flat opposite the sewage farm on the outskirts of town. He has no job, no education and not all that much confidence. He is not alone for long. In the pub one evening, he meets a girl, Tina. She is local, she is nice and soon she is pregnant.

A shotgun wedding follows. They walk up to the town hall to exchange vows. They have drinks with the two families and friends at the Social Club, with children chasing floating balloons on the hall floor. But there is no honeymoon. After the wedding, they settle down in his flat. But for both, marriage is not all that it is cracked up to be. Their baby girl is eager but noisy, hungry, demanding. Tina herself complains constantly – that he can't hold down a job, that he is not bringing in income.

One day though, he builds a coop in the yard and buys a chicken.

And by the end of one year, he has ten chickens.

By the end of two years, he has one hundred

chickens. By the end of three years, he has one thousand chickens. He is better off than he has ever been. Home life is good, Tina is content, his baby daughter is growing.

But then disaster strikes. One winter, the rains come down, harder and for longer than he could ever remember. The newspapers called it a record. The sewage farm floods. The sewage spreads across the road, into the yard and floods the coop. It kills all the chickens, who drown, and are left floating on the water for him to clear away.

One year later, he has no income, no job and no family, as Tina has left with his child, resettled across town. The father, now a grandfather, comes to the boy, now a young man. The father looks around the flat and sits down.

'Father,' says the young man, remembering what is was to be a boy. 'Look at my life. I have no money, no income, no job, no food, no family. You said that the politician was wrong to say that there is no alternative. You told me that there is always an alternative. Why has everything gone wrong?'

'Ah, but there was always an alternative, my son' the father replied.

'Ducks can swim. Chickens cannot. You should have bought a duck not a chicken. That was your alternative.'

20

The days of the wolf trial

Hamish Fyfe

The wooden shaft of the axe burnt in the woodcutter's hand as he sliced it down towards the wolf's head. Doing so their eyes met, locked in loathing and wonder. Just then, the woodcutter landed his axe with terrifying force inches away from the wolf's head, splitting the wood on which the animal lay entirely in two. The wolf and the man held their steady gaze with the force of centuries of mutual distrust and animus between their species. Neither flinched.

'I will spare you,' said the woodcutter, 'but only that human justice can be done and your fate decided by the laws of men.' The heart of the wolf sank at this, preferring, at that moment, to die honourably at the hand of his enemy than to be subject to human justice, which his species had come to distrust for as long as they had lived uneasily beside each other.

The wolf remained free from the cringing dependency forced on his cousins the dogs. The dignity of this ancient freedom coursed through his angry veins.

Reaching for a rope, the woodcutter tied the Wolf and – as he did so – it appeared to shrink to that of an animal half its size. The sinew and muscle, which had been so powerful during their fight, became limp and the animal lay helpless. Separated from his pack and his kind, he was on his own now and at the mercy of the ways of human beings.

Placing his adversary carefully in the cart, the woodcutter began to pull it away towards the town. As the cart jolted painfully along the track the tightness of the animal's bonds loosened a memory of playing with his brothers and sisters in snow so cold that it would have killed most animals just to breathe it. There is no cold that can harm us, he thought. Suddenly the wolf felt within him a single shattering howl, but he would not give voice to it. Not yet.

Word of Little Red and her hapless grandmother had already reached the town. The arrival of the Wolf, the violator of the little girl and her grandmother, caused a great stir. The streets were lined with people who had come to shout 'shame' at the Wolf, and to see at close hand the shape of such wickedness. 'You and your kind have stolen our sheep for as long as there have been people here. Now this deliberate and cowardly attack on a little girl and an old lady! It's time you met with justice in the only language you Wolves understand,' a woman shouted, before lunging toward the cart in a vain attempt to strike the Wolf as it passed.

Arriving at the steps of the Police Station, the Wolf lay motionless in the cart like a boneless pelt. Three men, who were each armed and ready to shoot their weapons if the Wolf misbehaved, lifted him. The animal did not move, but his eyes burned a deep and angry amber amongst his matted fur.

The woodcutter explained to the Mayor, who was waiting with some impatience for their arrival, that he had spared the wolf and brought him for trial by human kind. Knowing that those who voted for him would be there, the Mayor made a short speech:

'My fellow townspeople, we have lived beside
these cunning and vicious creatures for too long.
And I tell you this; it's going to stop. Wolves are
murderers and rapists, they kill our sheep and we
have no work or food because of them. They are
bad, bad animals and, if I am re-elected, I will put
a stop to them so that they can harm us no longer.
No wolf will be allowed to pass into these town

lands to terrorise us. I will make sure of it.'

At this the wolf was pulled unceremoniously from the cart and taken to a secure area at the back of the police station. The people who had come to see him would not see him again until the trial.

Little Red and her grandmother were well cared for in the days before the trial. They were kept in a safe house not far from the court, in case Wolves mounted a further attack on them. However, some people could be heard whispering about Little Red not being looked after properly by her mother. 'How could she send that poor little girl into the forest alone?', 'Oh well, it's the wolves' fault; you just can't trust them!' said others.

On the day of the trial, what seemed like the whole town was in the courtroom. People pushed each other aside to get the best view of the proceedings. Outside people carried placards and banners saying things like 'Hang the Wolf', 'Women against Wolves', and 'We want our town back'.

Crowding into the wooden bowl of the courtroom, the people could see lawyers and the Mayor, who had appointed himself judge of this important case, straightening papers and conferring with each other with pre-trial urgency. The Wolf, against all legal advice, had chosen to defend himself.

'Wolf,' announced the Judge. 'You are accused of attacking an old woman and her granddaughter with the intention of killing them and eating them. How do you plead?'

Not looking up from the ground to which his eyes were fixed, the wolf mumbled: 'Not guilty.'

'No, no, no, you must reply "Not guilty *your Honour*" or you will be in contempt of this court,' said the judge. A ripple of approval ran around the courtroom until the judge tapped his gavel on the bench in irritation.

The Wolf stood in determined and defiant silence. 'Very well we will continue with a plea of not guilty and deal with contempt later. Bring forward the first witness.'

Little Red looked very small in the huge wooden witness box. 'How old are you little girl?' the judge enquired, with a noticeably softer tone than before,

'I am eight,' said Little Red.

'And you live with your mother? How did you come to be in the woods that day?'

'My mother sent me with food for my grandmother who is old and ill.'

'Where exactly does your grandmother live?'

'On the edge of the forest, Sir,' said the little girl.

'And did you go straight there?'

'No. I stopped for a while and picked flowers for

my Grandma.'

'Wolf, did you follow Little Red and watch her as she picked the flowers?'

'Yes,' said the Wolf.

'Then why, if you were intent on killing, did you not do so then?'

The wolf made a sullen growl and said, coldly: 'I knew the little one would lead me to bigger prey. I am not hunting for myself but for my pack, we share our food. The territory of humans has got bigger and bigger and we are forced to hide in the woods rather than live in the broad valleys where we can hunt freely. More and more humans are using more and more land for timber, for grazing, for shooting and as farmland. Soon there will be no room left for us.'

'So your intention is to occupy as much territory as possible and to make it your own?'

Taking a deep but unsteady breath, the Wolf gathered himself to speak:

'Mr Mayor and people of the Town. We wolves are a proud species, I know, but we don't want to rule or conquer anyone. Human beings have that desire not us. Human greed has poisoned men's minds and has walled you inside new barriers of your own making. You humans are clever but your cleverness is unkind and harsh. You feel too little and think too much. We wolves live by each other's happiness – not by each other's misery. We don't want to hate and despise one another, as humans seem to. Wolves can be harsh when they are hungry, we will take the young, the vulnerable and the sick but we do this to live – we feel no hatred. Only the unloved can truly hate and as I stand here today I can feel the hatred that my difference from you brings. I could no more relinquish my wolf-hood and change my ways than you could your humanity. You have choice in what you do. I do not.

So, Mr Mayor, you can enslave me, you can take away my dignity, even take away my life but all you will be left with is the dead body of a wolf not an obedient animal. I am a father, a brother and a member of a pack. My kind have been part of your world for thousands of years and all we ask is to share it with you – in peace.'

When the Wolf had finished, nobody spoke and there was a moment of silence. Into the silence, the Wolf gathered himself reaching his full height, threw back his head and howled the eternal howl of all his kind. After what seemed a long time, the hushed and still crowd in the courtroom could hear, in the far distance, another howl. Piercing the ether, the song of the two wolves came together and formed a perfect arc of sound between them. In that moment, the people were listening to the wordless and ancient secrets of the world and they were struck with awe. The wolf was not alone and never would be.

The courtroom fell into a deep hush.

Eventually, as feet could be heard shuffling uncomfortably on the courtroom floor, the judge banged his gavel hard on the bench. Turning to the jury, he coughed loudly to give himself more time to think and instructed them to go away and consider a verdict.

After a long time had passed, the jury returned and the foreman stood to give the verdict.

'Your Honour,' he said. 'We have deliberated for a long time and we apologise for keeping you all. The jury took time to consider a verdict and, in light of the testimony of the Wolf, we went on to consider what action we could take to avoid this happening again.'

'And what conclusions did you come to?'

'Some felt that things had got so bad we should arm ourselves and our children at all times to keep ourselves safe. Some felt we should build a high wall around the boundary of the town to keep them out, but we know how good the wolves are at digging. Some of the jurors suggested that we should build a compound to keep them in where they could pursue their own ways and culture without hindrance. However, they would not be able to leave the compound. We suggest electric fences. Others felt that the only way to deal with the wolves was to reduce their numbers to such a point that they no longer pose a threat. Remaining wolves could live in the town zoo with an appropriate level of security. One juror felt we should keep the Wolf alive in separate confinement because of the danger of his becoming seen to be a martyr by other wolves.'

'These are all sensible measures and careful thought will be given to them by me as the election draws closer. However, we must now turn to the matter of the verdict. '

The foreman spoke again. 'Having given careful consideration to this case, we the jury find the Wolf guilty of intent to murder both Little Red and her Grandmother. The verdict was unanimous.'

'Thank you, members of the jury,' said the Mayor, as the crowd broke into raucous applause.

'I will clear this court if there is another outburst,' said the Mayor. Reaching for his black cap, which had not been used for a very long time, he spoke slowly and clearly: 'In the light of the jury's verdict, I sentence you to be hanged by the neck until dead, partly to rid ourselves of a murderous monster and partly to encourage others of your kind to stay away from us here, where they are not welcome. If, however, you agree to respect this court and address me in the proper way as 'Your Honour', I will reconsider the death sentence and you will be kept as a living exhibit in our zoo until such time as you die of natural causes. What do you say Wolf?'

The Wolf was quiet for a while and then said: 'I will not surrender my freedom and, in defence of it, I will accept any suffering. Do as you will with me.'

The people in the court shuffled quietly, many of them looking at the floor as they left the courtroom in troubled silence. The Wolf met his fate the next day.

21

Promise

Anna Jonsson,

(with Andrew Simms)

Once upon a time, it must have been towards the end of the last the century, many highways were to be built in the city of Stockholm. Then people learned about the how pollution from the vehicles that would fill the highways was dangerously unsettling the climate. They also knew that when you built new highways, far from curing congestion, roads just filled up with more traffic.

But, despite all this knowledge and understanding, and the layer of dust from construction and exhaust fumes that settled over the old planners' dreams as years passed, almost all those highways were built.

There was just one left (or to tell the truth, two, but for the sake of our tale we'll worry about the second another time). This missing highway was to be built in the eastern part of the city. A stretch of it would be sent underground in a tunnel below

Djurgården, a place where the oldest oaks still thrived in the city, and the owl still nested in peace.

Over the years, many people protested against the highways. But, time after time the voices of protest were brushed aside by politicians, who promised to keep future generations in mind, and another highway was built. The Department of Transport was an unstoppable machine – like one of those giant rollers, steadily, inexorably flattening the ground to lay the foundations of the next road.

They never thought to count what was lost, that was never part of the cost. Many even believed still that building roads would free them from traffic jams. Even though every time a new road appeared, it somehow magically filled with more cars and vans and lorries, until things were as bad as ever.

Then, one day in 2017, a thrilling, flourishing day in May, the head of the transport department – let us call him Mr T – was about to inspect the latest plans. His daughter, Emma, had a day off in school and went with him. She was a young woman who had a secret energy. She didn't talk much, but everyone seemed to notice her. What marks her out in our tale is that she knew about the *Promise*.

What promise, you say? It was one made so long ago that everyone else had forgotten it. But perhaps people also chose to forget the promise, because it became, well, inconvenient.

Back when most people made their living from the land, to get by, and sometimes just to survive, they relied upon the help of those who were hard to describe. They dwelt in the forest, and weren't people, or animals or dreams, but something else, real enough. They were many and varied and because people didn't really understand them, they called them all sprites, as in spirits, but rhyming with fright.

A promise was made to the sprites in the forest, when people left their daily work with the earth to search for something else (they told themselves it was happiness) in the city.

One of the sprites, the *tomte* (you may know it as an elf) provided help that went mostly unnoticed with the daily hard work on the land. It was feeding the cattle or cleaning the stable when the farmer was ill, always without showing its existence. But the tomte could also be harsh. If people were cruel to animals or forgot to put out a plate of porridge at the stair in front of the house at Christmas, the tomte could be mean and vengeful.

They were not to be taken for granted, and the tomte asked for a promise when the people left for the city. They were never to forget the sprites of the forest, including the *Näcken, skogsrå, småtomtan,* and vittren, or its creatures, the squirrels, the wolves, the beetles, the elks and the chaffinch. The people agreed and promised they would not forget.

Time passed and people had such a hard time surviving in the city, that the memory of the promise was forgotten. That is, by everyone except Emma. You remember her, don't you? As a small child, she spent summers with her grandmother, who was old enough to be still marked by the years of carrying water for the cattle and doing the laundry by the river in wintertime.

Small girls had the ability to see the tomte, trolls and the other sprites of the forest. In her childhood, Emma's grandmother could see them and they spoke to her as well, often asking her about the Promise. Did people remember? It didn't seem like it to them. So the old woman told her granddaughter all about it, and Emma kept this as a secret, and she knew that, some time, it would be important.

Emma never thought about the work her father did. She just knew that he left their house each day to go to his job, as most parents do.

So on this particular, thrilling day in May, she was curious. When Emma arrived in the Djurgården, and instantly, with a chill that both scared and excited her, she sensed the presence of sprites. She rushed to her father who, wearing a yellow hard hat and high visibility jacket, was striding around officiously waving plans in the company of surveyors and civil servants. As well as she could, Emma tried to tell her father about what she sensed, and about the Promise. She told him about Grandmother's words, and said that it would be insane to build a highway here, or anywhere for that matter. What about her future?

Distracted, he brushed her away, politely but firmly. He was busy with serious work. When she persisted, he just shrugged and tried to laugh her away: 'You have listened to your grandmother far too much, that is for sure!'

For the rest of the day Emma played by the trees while the men in yellow jackets and hats planned and talked and drank their coffee.

That night, Emma couldn't sleep. She lay in her bed, and looked out at the light spring night outside her window. Suddenly she heard light, quick steps running over the floorboards. Looking up, she saw a small tomte. He was no taller than a hand, with grey woollen clothes and a red beanie hat.

They both froze for a few seconds, one out of surprise and one from fear. Then the small tomte gathered all his courage, and made his feet tip-tap right up to Emma's bed. She helped him up on to the duvet, and let him whisper something in her ear. She nodded and then he ran away as fast as he had appeared.

Next day, when her father was on his way to work, he found an old watch in his pocket. It was a long time ago since he'd seen the pocket watch, which had been his father's, who passed away a few years before. All day, Emma's father could not stop thinking about the watch. It reminded him of when he played as a child and he thought about the tough times his father and grandparents endured when they were poor farmers.

He also came around to thinking about Emma; what now would her future be like? When she grew up, how would she look back on her own childhood, and what would her memories of him be like? And what about her children and grandchildren; in what kind of world would they be born, fall in love and die?

On the next night, Emma couldn't sleep again. Nervous but excited, she wanted to hear the small footsteps again. And, just as before, in the middle of the night she heard them, sudden and quick. The small tomte once again whispered to her, and again she smiled and nodded.

In the morning, her father was in a good mood. It

was a sunny day as he got ready to leave for work. He reached for his mobile phone in his pocket, but instead, this time, he found a small seed. It was so small, like a black dot in his hand, that he could barely see it. He thought about how extraordinary it was that such a small seed could grow into a huge tree or a beautiful flower. All day, he struggled to focus on his work, all his thoughts drifted, as if they wanted to escape, and run away to dwell on the mysteries of life.

The third night, Emma was prepared and, yes, the tomte came. He whispered. She nodded. And the third morning, her father went off to work. This time, he deliberately searched in his pocket (his work started to bore him, and his pocket started to interest him). This time, he found a small pocket mirror. He opened the lid and, in front of him, a face appeared that he scarcely recognised. It had grey hair and deep dark eyes surrounded by countless fine wrinkles. In those eyes, he saw a small boy as well as an old man. He saw time running out of his hands. And he started to think of his memory, the memory of him the world would have when he passed away.

That day, Emma´s father didn't go to work. He went to her school, catching her before she went in, he hugged her tightly and said: 'Yes, you are right, my child. Of course. How could I forget?'

You are probably now wondering what happened to the highway? Well, that is something that each and every one of us now living will decide.

22

Hinterland

Corrina Cordon

'When you have come to understand the true nature of rivers, you will realise that you have no further questions.'
Seneca

Once upon a time, not so very long ago, there was a girl named Freya. She lived on an estuary island at the mouth of a long and mighty river that flowed from the deep heart of the country into the cold, wild North Sea.

She shared a small house with her Mother and Father and a low fence separated their garden from the neighbours, who had a boy called Tommy of the same age. Freya, Tommy and the birch tree, which stood between their houses, grew together – their friendship as solid and unshakable as its roots.

When they were still very young and the tree little more than a sapling, they constructed a magic shrine at its base, a mound scraped together and mounted with a yellow plastic castle and flag. Here they would bring the treasures they had foraged from their various expeditions – an acorn, a silver button, a blackbird's feather – and solemnly place them in a tin provided by Freya's mother, secured in the ground as their own precious, personal vault.

As the seasons passed and the children grew, the little shrine gradually became neglected, replaced by homework and television and other more pressing activities, but it remained there, solidly indifferent to sun, rain and snow, it's secrets as deep and old as the earth.

Then a terrible darkness unexpectedly fell upon Freya's family. Her beloved father left the house one spring morning to go sea fishing and never returned. Lost at sea, her Mother said, clutching the jumper last worn by her husband, winding the sleeve tightly round her hand.

'But Mum, we can find him then,' said Freya, her sadness tightly bound in hope. That evening, she sat with Tommy beneath the birch tree, excavating their long buried treasures and placing them in a semi-circle around them. She wished to whatever gods and goddesses they had invoked in half-remembered ceremonies that her father would return before meticulously placing each object back in its chamber.

Months went by. The summer was long past and the air ripe with autumn, bonfires and decay. Her Mother's sharp grief was replaced by weary sadness and the teachers at Freya's school stopped asking how she was. Life continued much as it had before but viewed through a filter of grey as dark as the clouds that shadowed the sun.

Not long before Hallowe'en, a rumour gripped the town. Strange sounds had been heard, echoing across the estuary, disturbing late night dog walkers and young lovers. Sightings of a man were reported, moving among the marshes, roaming the space between land and sea. The children terrified themselves with tales of hideous monsters whilst the adults spoke of rising crime and unwanted immigrants. Parents, anxious to accompany their children safely home, greeted them at the school gates with unwelcome, embarrassing embraces.

Freya, an inquisitive child, was unusually attentive to the news. She had her reasons and hugged them close to her heart.

That evening, the two children cycled furiously through the twilight, shadowed by the concrete expanse of the sea wall rising above them. Built after the great flood of 1953, it stood to protect those within from the high tides of future storms. Or so the men who built it hoped.

The night was drawing close as the fog rolled in from the sea, creeping across the Essex marshland, conquering all in its path. Freya stopped suddenly and climbed the iron steps set into the wall, Tommy reluctantly following her down to the other side. In her haste, she stumbled and fell, landing in a heap on the other side. A sharp bolt of pain pierced her foot as she tried to stand. Blinking away tears, she conceded defeat.

'Oh Tommy, it really hurts. You'll have to go back and tell my Mum.'

'But what about... you know?'

'There's no-one here. I'll be alright, honest'.

Minutes passed slowly. Five, ten. In more usual circumstances, her lively mind would find it easy to while away the time, but in the cold, murky silence, she was reluctant to imagine too much.

A sound filled the air, echoing over the marshes, a long, deep note, full of sadness and longing. Foghorn from a boat perhaps but no, too close to come from the river. Twice and then three times, and between each blast, the unmistakable noise of footsteps squelching in the mud. The clouds parted as the watery light of the full moon illuminated the stranger that stood before her.

Freya's heart, thumping so loud she thought he must surely hear it, stared at the peculiar figure.

Matted, shoulder length fair hair, weathered face half covered by a moustache and beard heavily encrusted with sea salt, reaching almost to his chest. Around his shoulders was a cape of heavy wool and fur, almost concealing a long, rough woollen shirt and trousers tucked into leather boots.

The small, helpless girl fought her fear and disappointment as he looked to her with a distant, confused expression. The strangeness of his demeanour, dislocated as he was from his surroundings, dampened Freya's initial unease. He turned back towards the water, scanning the dark horizon.

She counted the beats of her pounding heart and on reaching one hundred, could bear the silence no more.

'Are you lost?' He gave no sign of recognition, so louder now, 'Excuse me, I said: are you lost?' Slowly he turned and looked down, acknowledging her presence for the first time.

'I am waiting.'

'What are you waiting for? It's getting late you know.'

'I am waiting for my ship.'

'What happened to it? You can sit down if you want. Maybe my friends can help when they get here.'

He contemplated for a moment before sitting.

'What is your name, child?'

'Freya. What's yours?'

Happiness fleetingly crossed his face. He leant in towards her and she nervously shifted back as best she could.

'I am sorry, I did not mean to scare you, but your name, I have not heard spoken in many years. You are from the northlands?'

'I'm from here, in Essex, but my Dad is from Sweden. I mean, he was, but he died.'

Freya began to cry, her small body wracked with belated grief. Looking up, she was surprised to see this strange man also weeping, tears rolling down his cheeks, forming small, shining pools in his beard.

'I'm sorry. I didn't mean to make you sad. It's all right. I wish he was still here though. I hoped you might be him, that's why we came here, me and my friend Tommy. I'll in real trouble when my Mum gets here. What's your name?'

'Olin.' His broad shoulders heaved and his voice was heavy with melancholy.

'What are you doing here?'

'I am waiting for my ship to return. This island was to be the last stop on our journey before returning home. We had sailed down the coast, stopping at towns where we could in search of food and gold. We put ashore and I left my crew to walk inland. When I came back, it had gone. I have been waiting for it to return to take me home.'

'How long have you been here?' asked Freya, only half wanting to hear the answer.

'I cannot say for sure. Perhaps a day. Perhaps a thousand years.' Freya, suppressing her growing unease and moved to pity for this lonely man, reached across to place a hand on his back and felt only the night breeze as it passed straight through him.

'But you're a...!' cried Freya, her words carried away by the wind.

'I do not know what I am. I have lost the people I love and the land that I know. And now I can only roam the in-between places, on the edge of the world. Can you imagine what it is to be far from home, away from your people, your family, with no chance of returning? It is part of who you are, and I did not understand what it was to belong, until I did not.'

Freya felt as if her tender heart could break for his loneliness. She wished more than anything that she could do something to help, for whether he was of this world or not, the sorrow of his loss was as real as hers.

An idea struck her. Reaching for the rucksack, she

pulled out the small casket of childhood treasures. It was to have been a present for her father.

'I have something for you.' Carefully removing the lid, she began to display the contents in a semi-circle around Olin's feet. The acorn. The silver button. The blackbirds feather. The glass necklace that had been a birthday gift from her Mother. Finally, her most valued possession. A small golden charm, given to her by her Father, in the figure of a Viking ship.

Olin turned to Freya, his eyes wide with wonder and for the first time he smiled. Reaching to the ground, he picked up one of the tiny objects, closed his fingers around it and pressed it to his chest.

'Thank-you, Freya, for bringing me my ship. I think it is time for me to go now.'

And with that, this shadow of a man who had wandered between worlds for too long, finally found his way home.

Footsteps again, crashing on iron this time, as Tommy ran down the stairs and her Mother gathered Freya in her arms.

In the back seat of the car, Tommy turned to his friend and whispered: 'Who were you talking to down there? I heard you when we was walking up.'

'Just someone who was lost, but I helped him and it's alright now.'

'I'm sorry you didn't find your Dad.'

'That's OK. I know he's not coming back, I just didn't want to admit it 'cos that would make it real. But it'll be better now. Let's go home.'

23

Those were dreams.
These are plans.
David Cross

The initial situation
We start with you.
It's all about you.
Made by you.

Make the future.
The future is now.
Now is calling.

I.   A family member absents themselves from home.
Go on.
Let's go forward.
Keep it moving.
Onwards.

II. An interdiction is addressed to the hero.
Do what you can't.

Don't crack under pressure.
Don't go there. Live there.
Don't leave home without it.

Love it. Hate it. Just don't forget it.

III. The interdiction is violated.

IV. The villain makes an attempt at reconnaissance.
Which one will you get?
What do you feel like?
When was the last time you felt really good about your skin?
Why not?

V. The villain receives information about his victim.
Love is out there. Search on.

VI. The villain attempts to deceive his victim.
We care because you do.

VII. The victim submits to deception and unwittingly helps his enemy.
Turn on your adventure.
See whatever you want to see.

Keep reinventing.

My mutant brain.

VIII. The villain causes harm.
When light meets dark.
There will be haters.

IX. Misfortune or lack is made known.
Something missing?
Bring something extraordinary.

X. The seeker agrees to, or decides upon
counteraction.
Listen to your instinct.
It's what connects us.

XI. The hero leaves home.
Go lighter, go longer.
Wander not wonder.
Own the journey.
Journey to your dream.
Stop dreaming. Start working.
Keep walking.

XII. The hero is tested.
Take the challenge.
See what's next.
Make it happen.

Live for now.

XIII. The hero reacts.
Cool. Calm. Connected.
Nothing to prove.

XIV. The hero acquires the use of a magical agent.
Unexpectedly powerful.
Power to you.
The power of dreams.
Practically magic.
Even angels will fall.

XV. The hero is led to the object sought.
Be there.
Anywhere. Effortlessly.
Go further.
Go further to get closer.
Why not?

XVI. The hero and villain join in combat
Beautiful things are worth fighting for.
Strong is beautiful.
Choose beautiful.
A world with no heroes.
It's what's happening.

XVII. The hero is branded.
Defy labels.
Falling is the first step to rise.
Luxury makes a difference.
It's not just who we listen to. It's who we are.

XVIII. The villain is defeated.
No blood should hold us back.

XIX. The initial misfortune or lack is liquidated.
Because acting quickly can make all the difference.
There's always a way to make life better.
Rush less, feel more.

XX. The hero returns.
Return with something to declare.

XXI. The hero is pursued.
Because sometimes happiness is in the journey as
well as the destination.

XXII. Rescue of the hero from pursuit.
Seduction never ends.
Never stop. Never settle.

XXIII. The hero, unrecognised, arrives home.
Greatness awaits.

XXIV. A false hero presents unfounded claims.
Good goes round.
It doesn't just tell time. It tells history.
Now you can please both head and heart.
Watch the impossible become unimpossible.

XXV. A difficult task is proposed to the hero.
Commit to something.
Find your greatness.
Make it happen.
Give the rainbow.

XXVI. The task is resolved
When the unexpected happens, expect the best.
Everything managed.

XXVII. The hero is recognised
Find yourself.
Proud to make a difference.
One in a billion.
Winning tastes good.

XXVIII. The false hero or villain is exposed
Colour as real as you are.

XXIX. The hero is given a new appearance.
Pow! De-ageing for the impatient.

See the wonderful.
The gift of beauty.

XXX. The villain is punished.
Never hide.
It's good to be bad.

XXXI. The hero is married and ascends the throne.
It's what you do in the dark that puts you in the
light.
Tomorrow is overrated.
Create a better tomorrow tonight.

Come together.
Be together. Not the same.
Best Alone, Better Together.
Believe in Better.

Note

The above piece presents in italics recent English language advertising and marketing slogans within the 'syntagmatic' structure articulated by Vladimir Propp in *Morphology of the Folktale* (1928), translated by Laurence Scott (Austin and London: University of Texas Press, 1968).

Key

The initial situation
    Currys/PC World
    Clarins
    Converse
    Shell
    Renault
    Audi

I. A family member absents themselves from home.
    Hovis
    Barclays
    Smirnoff ice
    HSBC

II. An interdiction is addressed to the hero.
    Samsung
    TAG Heuer
    Airbnb
    Amex
    Marmite

III.   The interdiction is violated.

IV. The villain makes an attempt at reconnaissance.
    McDonald's

Cadburys
Nurture
Easyjet

V. The villain receives information about his victim.
Google

VI. The villain attempts to deceive his victim.
Lenor

VII. The victim submits to deception and unwittingly helps his enemy.
Volkswagen
Jeep
Hewlett Packard
Kenzo

VIII. The villain causes harm.
Desperados
Adidas

IX. Misfortune or lack is made known.
Royal British Legion
Grey Goose vodka

X. The seeker agrees to, or decides upon counteraction.

Aura Mugler
HBO

XI. The hero leaves home.
Nike
Boohoo
Strongbow
Danone
Nike
Johnnie Walker

XII. The hero is tested.
Colgate
Microsoft
RBS
Pepsi

XIII. The hero reacts.
VW Tiguan
Audi

XIV. The hero acquires the use of a magical agent.
Bosch
Vodafone
Honda
Apple
Lynx

XV. The hero is led to the object sought.
BT Sport
Uber
Ford
British Airways
Easyjet

XVI. The hero and villain join in combat.
Audi
Pantene
Dove
Ubisoft
Twitter

XVII. The hero is branded.
Mini Clubman
Band Aid
Jacob Cohën
YouTube

XVIII. The villain is defeated.
Libresse Bodyform

XIX. The initial misfortune or lack is liquidated.
HSBC
Philips
Galaxy

Air sorted

XXVII. The hero is recognised.
   River Island
   SSE
   Adidas
   Mars

XXVIII. The false hero or villain is exposed,

XXIX. The hero is given a new appearance.
   Clinique
   Pandora
   Boots

XXX. The villain is punished.
   Ray Ban
   Jaguar

XXXI. The hero is married and ascends the throne.
   Under Armour
   Jose Cuervo
   Absolut
   H&M
   Android
   Young & Rubicam
   Sky

24

The fox and the buzzard

Deborah Rim Moiso

*(translated from the original Italian
by Matt Rendell)*

What had become of the river water?

Everyone was wondering. The oak pushed its roots down, down into the depths, through the layers of earth and rock, but couldn't find it. The apple tree stretched its branches out further and further, but couldn't find it.

What had become of the river water?

The flocks of starlings flew in wider and narrower circles, but couldn't find it. The animals that ran, jumped and crawled looked for it, but couldn't find it.

The wild boar got organised: they had collected the plastic buckets that the humans leave all over the woods and they formed a convoy to go and bring water from the regions nearby.

The frogs croaked.

What had become of the river water?

The wolves had gone.

What had become of the river water?

So it carried on for an age, or a moment – the story doesn't say – until the animals in the woods, exhausted, decided the call the Great Assembly. They gathered in a clearing beside the dry river, between the oak and the apple tree, beneath the thick foliage.

They discussed all night. All day, and all night, until, on the night of the full moon, they reached their decision: they would send an emissary to the humans, because the humans were quick. They used their heads. And because, as the crow put it, there was no doubt that it was all their fault.

So who do you think they sent?

Many animals were considered for the task, in the end the Assembly chose the fox. And the fox, deeply flattered, accepted the task and set off. She crossed the dry river, reached the chestnut trees at the limits of the woods, looked in her heart and saw that she was afraid. She turned around and said: 'I certainly can't go and speak to the humans in this condition.'

She went to the bird's barber shop and tidied up her hair, buffed up her tail, combed the tuft over her ears and then, with much more confidence, set off again along the path.

There is a goddess in me /There is a garden in me /There is a star in me /There is a galaxy in me,
Look at me, look /Look at me, look / Look at me, look ...

She set off, across the dry river, reached the edge of the woods and the chestnut trees and, when she was more or less half way along the road that led across the hill to the village, she looked in her heart and saw that she was afraid. She doubled back along the path, gave two big blows to the drum with her big tail, all buffed up and perfumed, and said: 'I can hardly go like this! I need at least to take a gift for when I appear before the Meeting of Men.'

The Assembly saw that she was right, and they gave her fire.

The fox took it and set off across the dry river and the chestnut grove and, when she reached the top, before the walls of the village, she looked in her heart and saw that she was afraid. She turned around and sad: 'No. I can't go in alone.'

In the woods, the Assembly saw that she was right. They decided to send someone with her. Many animals were considered. In the end, they chose the buzzard, the bird of prey that flies high up in the sky.

*The divine is in you /A dense forest is in you
/Treasure is within you /There is a universe in
you.
Can you hear me? Listen /Can you hear me?
Listen Listen. Can you hear me?*

The buzzard agreed, and they set off again. The
fox crossed the dry river, the chestnut glade and
reached the gates of the village, while the buzzard
flew above her, in wider and wider, then narrower
and narrower circles, looking over her.

Finally, the fox and the buzzard entered the
village walls, high on the hill. Now, those were the
days of the village feast, so the first thing the fox saw
when she stepped inside the old gate and crossed the
threshold into Collalto – for so the village was called
– was tables and tables of people eating and
drinking. Bread rolls, brimming glasses, and huge
plates full of food being carried left, right and centre.

Straight away, the fox began to eat the discarded
food beneath the table. Distracted, she forgot why
she had come, until the buzzard, perched on the
highest rampart of the castle, threw a small stone
that hit her right in the small of her back.

'Ouch!' said the fox. She left the morsel, looked
around, heard the call of the buzzard who had taken
off again and was flying high among the clouds. Then

she remembered why she had come, and set off again. Continuing through the village streets, the next thing the fox saw was a great dance floor. To cross it and reach the other side, she would have to negotiate through all the movement and confusion, with legs intertwined and feet that rose and fell to unfamiliar rhythms. What was she to do? Straight away the fox thought: 'Easy. From above, the buzzard will be able to show me the path across.' She looked up into the sky by the buzzard had disappeared.

The fox looked into her heart and saw that she was afraid. She took a deep breath and took a moment to think. She considered her predicament. She looked around attentively, listened carefully, tried to understand what was going on. After an age, or a moment – the story doesn't say – she understood how to cross from one side to the other without being seen. And that is what she did.

But what was the fox looking for? The fox was looking for the Meeting of Men. But the men have forgotten how to hold a proper Assembly. There was nothing in the neighbourhood that looked like an Assembly she recognised. Then, around a corner of flowering jasmine and Helichrysum, in a little square with a well at the centre, the fox saw something that looked just like an Assembly. It was a group of people in a circle, who were talking and laughing and passing around a coloured object.

It wasn't exactly the same as an Assembly, of course. And the people were smaller than the other people. But the fox thought it might do: she observed them attentively, summoned all her courage, and entered the circle of children who were playing with a ball. Immediately, the buzzard, gliding down from on high, far higher than the highest tower in the castle, flew down and landed in the centre of the circle with her.

There is a goddess in me /There is a garden in me /The divine is in you /A dense forest is in you. Look for me look /Look for me look /Look, you are looking for me.

The fox and the buzzard explained the situation to the children, who immediately understood and decided to send a little boy and a little girl to the Great Assembly in the Woods, to see what could be done. The little girl, whose name was Antara, had long red hair entwined with ivy. The little boy was a bit tubby, but courageous and strong, His name was Antonio.

There is a star in me /There is a galaxy in

me/Treasure is within you /There is a universe
in you.
Look for me look /Look for me look /Look, you
are looking for me...

Walking behind the fox and with the buzzard
flying high in the sky, Antaro and Antonio went
down the path into the woods, crossed the chestnut
glade and the dry river and reached the Assembly of
the animals. They were there a long time, talking and
learning many things. Their mission was discussed
for a day, a night and a day until, in the end, during a
moonless night, the time came to leave. They were to
go far and find the river water.

Go, seek, collect and return. Go, seek, return and
tell the story.

The children said: 'Don't send us like this, empty
handed.' So the fox approached them and said: 'Of
course. Here: I have brought you fire, to warm you
and light the path. And I can give you my tail too, my
beautiful, thick tail.'
And the buzzard said: 'I can give you my feathers.'

There is a whole world in me /There is fire and
water in me /Roots and leaves in me /There is

earth and sky in me.
Touch me touch /Touch me touch /Touch you are
touching me...

Antara looked at the Assembly. She looked at Antonio, who was travelling with her. She looked at the fire, the fox's tail the buzzard's feathers, and she said: 'It is not enough.'

The children readied themselves to leave. But, before they left, they returned home to speak with their parents. Antara spoke with her father, Antonio with his mother. They talked for a long time. It was hard to let them go.

Go, seek, collect and return. Go, seek, return and tell the story.

In the end, their parents agreed to let them leave. And, before they left, they met under a lime tree, in the centre of the village, to say farewell and to sing.

The apple tree

Go, seek, collect and then come back.
Go, seek, return and tell the story.

Stay with me
I will give you a house and walls to live in
I leave because
I want space around me

Stay with me
I will give you a field and an apple tree
I leave because
There is a road within me

If I give you a house, open the doors
If I give you a plant, hand out the fruit
If I give you silence, speak with everyone
I love it when you leave, I loved it when you
came back

Stay with me
I will give you a field and an apple tree
Stay because
Here I will die without you

I leave because
I am looking for a field with an apple tree
I leave because
Here I will die with you

If I give you a house, open the doors

If I give you a plant, hand out the fruit
If I give you silence, speak with everyone
I love it when you leave, I loved it when you came back

Stay with me
We will pick the fruit from the apple tree
Stay because
You want to dance with me

I leave because
Within me there is a field with an apple tree
I leave because
Your dance is within me

If I give you a house, open the doors
If I give you a plant, hand out the fruit
If I give you silence, speak with everyone
I love it when you leave, I loved it when you came back

I leave because
Within me there is a field with an apple tree
I leave because
Your dance is within me

Stay with me

We will pick the fruit from the apple tree
Stay because
You want to dance with me

Come with me
We will eat the fruit of the apple tree
Come with me because
You want to dance with me

Go, seek, collect and then come back.
Go, seek, return and tell the story.

25

The knock

Andrew Simms

Always timid, the event that led to Daniel's sudden sensory loss left him consumed with shame, and even more withdrawn from the world. On a freezing night in the city, hurrying home from work, he'd turned a corner to see a gang of boys pushing and kicking a homeless man. Outraged but fearful of confrontation, he'd stepped from the pavement to avoid the scene.

One of the gang saw him and sneered, making Daniel trip on the icy curb, and hit his head. The gang laughed, and the knock left him dizzy and his sense of smell and hearing suddenly gone. Doctors explained this was not unusual, that senses normally return, but they couldn't say when or give guarantees.

Daniel wasn't surprised, he knew he was the kind of person that life knocked, and just felt a little smaller and more angry with himself. At work they grudgingly adapted to his disabilities, but gave him more menial things to do. Returning home on Friday night after the first week in his now diminished world, seething but crushed, he was about to walk passed the new soup kitchen next to his home.

It was set up for homeless people, refugees and asylum seekers disallowed from work. A group quietly queued who looked Middle Eastern. Then Daniel saw the same gang from before approaching with menace, it was clear they intended to harm the people in the queue. Fear and outrage gripped him.

In an agony of indecision, Daniel grabbed a lamp post to steady himself. Internally raging against his inability to act, he hit his head in frustration hard against his hand holding the post, but then gathered every ounce of his strength, stepped suddenly towards the gang and, just before they launched an attack, screamed: 'Enough, enough, ENOUGH!' somehow making himself appear a lot larger than he was.

It was so unexpected, so sudden, and the pitch of his voice so unusual – shrill, steely and a little deranged – that the whole queue pitched round, sharply alert. The gang stopped in their tracks, looking at each other, and laughing nervously before drifting away in a slow swagger. Shocked at himself, exhausted in his sensory-deprived fog, Daniel stumbled to his front door and disappeared inside, watched silently but wide-eyed by the people at the soup kitchen.

He woke the next day still dazed and feeling wretched - about himself and the state of the world.

Then there was a knock at the door. And, very strangely, Daniel could hear it. He'd grown accustomed to silence and so was confused, but rushed sure-footedly to open it.

A kaleidoscope of floral aromas hit Daniel's reawakened senses, drifting from a huge bunch of flowers held by the delivery person. No one had ever given him flowers before and his mind raced, almost overcome.

'My hearing, the smell, it must have been that second blow,' he thought, as he opened a card which read, simply: 'Thank you, The Soup Kitchen.'

Biographies of the authors

David Boyle is a writer, 'think-tanker' and co-director of the New Weather Institute, and has been at the heart of numerous public policy innovations including the effort to develop co-production and introduce time banks to Britain as a critical element of public service reform. Reporting for the Cabinet Office, he was the coalition government's independent reviewer on the Barriers to Public Service Choice (2012-13). His book *Authenticity: Brands, Fakes, Spin and the Lust for Real Life* (2003) helped put the search for authenticity on the agenda as a social phenomenon. *The Tyranny of Numbers* (2001) predicted the backlash against the government's target culture. *Funny Money* (1999) launched the time banks movement in the UK. He also writes history books. Twitter: @davidboyle1958

Corrina Cordon was born in Essex and studied history at Sussex University. Her story was inspired by the bleakly beautiful Essex coastline and Canvey marshes that as a child she referred to as the end of the world. A ghostly Viking has been sighted there, looking for his ship to take him home. She lives in Forest Hill, London and works at Friends of the Earth, campaigning for a better, fairer world for people and the only planet we call home.

David Cross is an artist and academic, engaging with the contested ideal of sustainability in relation to visual culture. David graduated from St Martins School of Art in 1989. From 1991, when he left the Royal College of Art, until 2014, he collaborated with Matthew Cornford as Cornford & Cross, making context-specific art projects that addressed critical issues to activate social agency. Recognising a conflict between his internationalism and environmentalism, David stopped using jet travel in 2005. As a Reader at the University of the Arts London (UAL), David works for education as a public good, combining transformative pedagogy with constructive institutional critique.

Jan Dean is a poet-in-schools whose work appears in over a hundred anthologies. Her latest book is *The Penguin in Lost Property* – written with Roger Stevens (Macmillan). She is a National Poetry Day Ambassador for Forward Arts. Jan comes from the North West but now lives in Devon.

Sarah Deco is a storyteller based in London. She founded and co-runs the North London Traditional Storytelling Circle. She tells stories in schools and libraries, at festivals and retreats and other diverse venues. She was for many years an art therapist and group psychotherapist working in the NHS in mental health. She now facilitates workshops in personal and professional development using story. She is particularly interested in exploring myth and story in relation to environmental awareness and social change.

Her website is: www.sarahdecostoryteller.com

Suki Ferguson is a writer, facilitator, and social justice campaigner. She works at Quakers in Britain. She is the co-author of the New Economy Organiser Network Power & Privilege Guide. An advocate for the power of listening, she runs peer-to-peer coaching sets for campaigners, and gives tarot readings to the conflicted and the curious. She tweets at @SukiKF.

Hamish Fyfe is Professor of the Arts and Society at the University of South Wales. He is Director of the George Ewart Evans Centre for Storytelling which is the only research European research centre with storytelling as its focus. He is an Associate Editor of the *Journal of Arts and Communities.*

Jayati Ghosh is one of the world's leading economists. She is professor of economics at Jawaharlal Nehru University, New Delhi, and the executive secretary of International Development Economics Associates (www.networkideas.org). She writes for *The Guardian* in the UK, is a regular columnist for several Indian journals and newspapers, and author or editor of a dozen books, including, most recently, Demonetisation Decoded: A critique of India's monetary experiment (with Prabhat Patnaik and CP Chandrasekhar), and The Elgar Handbook of Alternative Theories of Economic Development (with Erik Reinert and Rainer Kattel). She has advised or been consulted by several governments and international organisation, is closely involved with a range of progressive organisations and social movements and has received six prizes for her research work. Her contribution to this volume is her first folk tale.

Anna Jonsson is a founder and member of the Swedish environmental cabaret group Sweet Dreams and a former chairwoman of Friends of the Earth Sweden. She works for the Green Party in the Swedish parliament, and has a passion for folk music, running in forests and the joy of play.

Anthea Lawson is a campaigner and writer. She started out as a journalist on *The Times'* graduate trainee scheme, until that got subverted by holidays on a permaculture project in Spain where she found some back copies of *New Internationalist* and started waking up. Since then she has been an arms trade researcher at Amnesty International and an aid worker in Sierra Leone. Until recently, she worked at the NGO Global Witness, where she published investigations showing how banks fuel corruption in poor countries, and launched an award-winning campaign for transparency in company ownership which, following hard graft by many other activists, resulted in new laws and an emerging global standard to prevent crooks and tax evaders hiding behind front companies. Now, she's still campaigning for environmental and economic justice, though she's also increasingly interested in the psychology of activism and social change.

James Marriott is an artist and activist who works as part of Platform (www.platformlondon.org). Within this collective he has co-created projects ranging from opera to a micro-hydro plant and co-authored several books including *The Oil Road:*

journeys from the Caspian Sea to the City of London (Verso, 2012) with Mika Minio-Paluello. Platform's current work includes: Unravelling the Carbon Web focused on the human rights and environmental impacts of oil & gas corporations, in particular BP and Shell, and seeking to bring about their rapid closure.

Ed Mayo is Secretary General of Co-operatives UK, the national association for co-operative and mutual enterprise. He is chair of the participation charity Involve, a Vice-President of Co-operatives Europe and formerly Chief Executive of the New Economics Foundation (1992-2003). Ed is author of *A Short History of Co-operation and Mutuality* (2017) and *Values: how to bring values to life in your business* (Routledge, 2016).

Bill McGuire is an academic, broadcaster and writer of popular science and speculative fiction. He is currently Professor Emeritus of Geophysical and Climate Hazards at University College London. Bill was a member of the UK Government Natural Hazard Working Group established in January 2005, in the wake of the Indian Ocean tsunami, and in 2010 a member of the Science Advisory Group in Emergencies (SAGE) addressing the Icelandic volcanic ash problem. In 2011, he was one of the authors of the IPCC report on climate change and extreme events. His non-fiction books include *A Guide to the End of the World: Everything you Never Wanted to Know* and *Surviving Armageddon: Solutions for a Threatened Planet* and, most recently, *Waking the Giant: How a Changing Climate Triggers Earthquakes, Tsunamis and Volcanoes.* He was consultant and main contributor to the BBC *Horizon* films; *Supervolcanoes* and *Megatsunami - Wave of Destruction*, as well as for the BBC drama, *Supervolcano.* Bill writes for *The Guardian, The Times* and *The Observer,* and is a regular contributor to *New Scientist* and *Focus* magazines. He recently co-presented *Project Doomsday* with comedy duo, Robin & Partridge. He lives, runs and grows fruit and veg in the Peak District, where he lives with his wife Anna, sons Jake and Fraser, and cats Dave, Toby and Cashew.

Geoff Mead is a storyteller, consultant, and the author of two books on the power of stories and storytelling: *Coming Home to Story: Storytelling Beyond Happily Ever After* (Vala, 2011) and *Telling the Story: The Heart and Soul of Successful Leadership* (Jossey-Bass, 2014). He is the founder of

Narrative Leadership Associates, a consultancy focused on the use of storytelling for sustainable leadership. As an organizational consultant, keynote speaker and workshop leader, he has taken his work on narrative leadership onto the shopfloors and into the boardrooms of blue chip companies, charities, universities and government departments, for the past two decades (www.narrativeleadership.com). Geoff performs traditional stories at International Festivals and storytelling clubs and runs story-based workshops in the UK and as far afield as Spain, Canada and Japan.

Marion Molteno is a prize-winning novelist whose work is inspired by contact with people of many different backgrounds. She was a policy advisor to Save the Children, supporting projects with vulnerable children in countries across Asia and Africa, and she founded the South London Refugee Project. Her latest novel, *Uncertain Light,* is set among people who work in humanitarian crises. She is an active grandmother, and can't understand why all parents and grandparents aren't concerned about what kind of earth we are leaving to our children. She blogs at http://www.marionmolteno.co.uk/my-blog/

Chris Nichols lives on Dartmoor. He's a long distance walker. Having recently walked the 1,000 km of the South West Coast Path, he's about to walk the borders and coasts of Wales. When he's not walking or getting to know his baby granddaughter, he is co-founder of the collaborative hub Gameshift.co.uk.

Jules Pretty is author of the recently published *The East Country: Almanac Tales of Valley and Shore* (Cornell University Press, 2017), and previously *The Edge of Extinction* (2014), and the award-winning *This Luminous Coast* (2011). He is Professor of Environment and Society at the University of Essex.

Nick Robins works in London on sustainable finance. He has been head of SRI funds at Henderson Global Investors and head of HSBC's Climate Change Centre. Currently he is co-director of UNEP's Inquiry into a Sustainable Financial System. He has published widely on sustainability issues and co-edited *Sustainable Investing: the Art of Long-term Performance*. He is also a historian and in 2006 published *The Corporation that Changed the World: How the East India Company Shaped the Modern Multinational.*

Andrew Simms is a political economist, environmentalist and co-founder of the New Weather Institute. He is a research associate at the Centre for Global Political Economy, University of Sussex, and a fellow of the New Economics Foundation (nef), where he was policy director for many years, running nef's work on climate change, energy and interdependence, and instigating their 'Great Transition' project. In work on local economies he coined the term 'clone towns' to describe the homogenization of high streets by chain stores. His books include *Tescopoly* and *Ecological Debt*. He co-authored *The New Economics, Eminent Corporations,* and the *Green New Deal*, devising the concept of 'ecological overshoot day' to illustrate when we begin living beyond our environmental means. Described by *New Scientist* magazine as "a master at joined-up progressive thinking", his latest book, *Cancel the Apocalypse: the New Path to Prosperity* is manifesto of new economic possibilities. Experimenting with new ways to tell the story of economics, he co-wrote, produced and performed *Neoliberalism: the Break-Up Tour*, with Sarah Woods. He tweets from: @andrewsimms_uk

Annes Stevens (*cover designer*) is an artist and illustrator with over eight years professional experience in the field of visual development. She has worked for industry-leading games studios EA Games and Lionhead and on prominent titles such as 'Harry Potter', 'Monopoly', 'Trivial Pursuits' and the award-winning 'Fable' franchise. She likes to develop new ideas and explore new styles, pushing visuals in a direction yet to be explored. Most recently, she has been working with Karrot Animation as art director on the new CBeebies animation series *Sarah & Duck*.

Katherine Trebeck is Senior Researcher for Oxfam GB where she is exploring steps towards a new economic paradigm. Her forthcoming book *Arrival* (co-authored with Jeremy Williams) advocates shifting notions of development from growth to quality and distribution as we seek to 'make ourselves at home' in a wealthy world. When working for Oxfam Scotland, Katherine developed the Humankind Index, a measure of prosperity constructed through community consultation, which she has explained in a TedX talk. Katherine has a PhD in political science from the Australian National University, is an Honorary Professor at the University of the West of Scotland, Senior Visiting Research Fellow at the University of Strathclyde, and was part of GIZ's Global Leadership Academy's New Economic Paradigm project. Katherine was a

Commissioner on the Fairer Fife Commission, sits on WWF Scotland's Low Carbon Infrastructure Task Force, and is Rapporteur for Club de Madrid's Working Group on Environmental Sustainability and Shared Societies.

Leslie Van Gelder is an archaeologist and writer living in the Rees Valley of New Zealand. She is the author of *Weaving a Way Home* and *The Archaeology of Love*. Her work focuses on the power of place in emotional landscapes. Her archaeological work in prehistoric finger flutings has helped to shed light on the lives of people who left their marks in caves twenty thousand years ago.

Sarah Woods is a writer, performer, activist and facilitator whose work has been produced by companies including the RSC, Hampstead, Soho Theatre and the BBC, along with regional theatres and touring companies. She works with communities, campaigns, scientists and specialists. Current work includes *Bordered* for BBC Radio 4, about human rights and the migrant crisis, a new opera *Lazarus* for Birmingham Opera, and The Centre for Alternative Technology's *Zero Carbon: Making it Happen* report. Sarah is narrative artist with Cardboard Citizens, who make theatre with and for homeless people. She teaches playwriting at Manchester University and is a Wales Green Hero.

**

New Weather Institute

We are a co-operative think-tank, focused on forecasting change and making the weather. We were created to accelerate the rapid transition to a fair economy that thrives within planetary boundaries. We bring together radical thinkers, scientists, economists, makers, artists and activists to find, design and advocate ways of working and living that are more humane, reasonable and effective.

Web: www.newweather.org
Twitter: @NewWeatherInst

The Real Press

The Real Press is a small, independent publisher, specialising in history books with an edge, a description broad enough to include this one.

Web: www.therealpress.co.uk
Twitter: @therealpresspub

By many of the same authors...

There was a knock
at the door...

23 modern folk tales for *troubling* times

Edited by Andrew Simms

Foreword by Philip Pullman

Printed in Great Britain
by Amazon